CRITICAL ACCLAIM FOR JANE ADAMS

The Greenway

'A haunting debut.' Minette Walters

'*The Greenway* lingered in my mind for days. It takes the psychological suspense novel into new realms of mystery.' Val McDermid, *Manchester Evening News*

'Adams's narrative has a simplicity that is misleading. The story is compellingly told and rich with psychological insight.' *Independent*

'An assured first novel, with a strong cast and a plot which twists and turns without a glitch.' *Yorkshire Evening Press*

Cast the First Stone

'Adams's debut last year, *The Greenway*, hinted at a promising crime-writing talent; *Cast the First Stone* amply confirms that view.' Marcel Berlins, *The Times*

'A powerful and corrosive thriller about child abuse, suspicion and guilt. Gripping, scary, a wonderful read. She could rise to the top of the genre.' *Yorkshire Post*

'The grippingly edgy quality of this *policier* . . . is taut-
ened almost unbearably.' *Sunday Times*

'Will keep you on the edge of your seat from the first
few pages until the chilling climax.' *Stirling Observer*

Bird

'Jane Adams' first two novels of psychological suspense
promised a major talent in the making. With *Bird* she
amply fulfils that promise with assurance and style.' Val
McDermid, *Manchester Evening News*

'The art of the truly great suspense novel, an art which
Adams has mastered.' *Crime Time*

'I am a great fan of good commercial fiction, and it rarely
comes better than Jane Adams' *Bird*. It is a haunting
crime novel and psychodrama pulling all the right strings
in all the right places.' *The Bookseller*

Fade to Grey

'Jane Adams has already carved herself a substantial
reputation for hauntingly resonant novels of psychological suspense.' *The Times*

'Jane Adams couldn't write a bad book if she tried . . . a
top-notch book by a rapidly maturing talent.' *Crime
Time*

'A cleverly constructed, slow-to-unravel crime mystery.'
South Wales Argus

'An intriguing thriller.' *North of Scotland Newspapers*

Final Frame

Jane Adams was born in Leicester, where she still lives. She has a degree in sociology, and has held a variety of jobs including lead vocalist in a folk rock band. She enjoys pen and ink drawing, two martial arts (Aikido and Tae Kwon Do) and her ambition is to travel the length of the Silk Road by motorbike. She is married with two children.

Final Frame is the fourth novel in the series featuring Detective Inspector Mike Croft and the direct sequel to *Fade to Grey*. In 1995 *The Greenway*, her debut novel, was nominated both for the Crime Writers' Association John Creasey Award for best first crime novel of 1995 and the Authors' Club Best First Novel award.

Jane Adams is also the author of *Bird*, a chilling ghost story now available in Pan Books. Her new novel, *The Angel Gateway*, will be published in Macmillan hardback in August 2000.

By the same author in Pan Books

The Greenway

Cast the First Stone

Bird

Fade To Grey

Final Frame

Jane Adams

PAN BOOKS

First published 1999 by Macmillan

This edition published 2000 by Pan Books
an imprint of Macmillan Publishers Ltd
25 Eccleston Place, London SW1W 9NF
Basingstoke and Oxford
Associated companies throughout the world
www.macmillan.co.uk

ISBN 0 330 37583 0

A CIP catalogue record for this book is available from
the British Library.

Phototypeset by Intype London Ltd
Printed and bound in Great Britain by
Mackays of Chatham plc, Chatham, Kent

For Chris Martin – sorry I didn't become a poet. For Tony Lawson, once of Newbiggen-on-Sea. Miss Shaw, who talked about Tolkien and JFK, and Mr Barnes, of New Parks House Junior '69/'70, who taught us that respect was a two-way street and that every one of us mattered.

And most of all for Kerry. Blessings.

Prologue

They had been forced to leave the car parked at the head of the lane and carry their equipment along the narrow track.

From the top of the hill they got a view across the valley for the first time, the high hedges either side of the road having blocked any sight of the landscape as they had driven up. It was a beautiful but claustrophobic place.

Liz pointed across to the opposite rise. 'That's the farm where we asked directions. See, it's marked on the map and this' – she nodded towards the house at the side of the lane – 'must be the Jacksons place.'

Macey nodded, swinging the camera bag across his shoulder. 'Through there,' he said, pointing to a narrow opening between the trees.

Neither spoke as they pushed their way along what was little more than a rabbit track through a tangle of trees and across a plank bridge over a tiny stream. They reached the second stile, beyond which was Forestry Commission land. Here, they both paused. Liz exchanged a glance with Macey, not needing to say a word. The tip-off had come in a couple of hours before. If this was for real then, they had a very good idea of who had brought them to this place and suddenly, being here, just the two of them, didn't seem too bright.

'Maybe we should have waited for the police,' Liz suggested tentatively.

Macey shook his head. 'And have them get here to find it's all a wind-up?'

Liz gave him a shrewd look. Macey didn't believe the hoax theory any more than she did. He just wanted to be there first, before the arrival of the local police pushed them back behind the usual barriers. Macey had followed every angle of the story as it had been reported in the nationals and now this had happened on his home ground. If it was for real, it could be his break into the big time.

Macey made the first move, handing his equipment to Liz while he eased himself over the stile, then helping her across. Behind them, the mixed woodland they had left was alive with the noise and rustling of wildlife. Here, in this dimly lit conifer plantation, there was an uncanny stillness.

'I don't like this place,' Liz whispered, expecting one of Macey's usual acerbic rejoinders. But for once the big man was silent.

They looked around. Behind them, the hill continued to rise, densely planted and very dark. The path itself was wider than it had been but dropped off to the right, falling down the hill into a steep gully.

Below, in the gully, there was only a chaos of fallen trees and deeply channelled earth eroded by last winter's rains. Liz looked again at the sketch map. This was definitely the place.

She and Macey began to scramble down. It took all their attention just to keep their footing and protect their camera equipment from being slammed against the rough ground and exposed roots. They did not see it until the trees thinned and the scene was suddenly there, exposed in all its terrible beauty.

The body lay, naked, on a rough bed of fallen branches and fresh flowers. All around, on every low branch, every niche that could be used, stood tiny candles, their white stems gleaming in the flickering light.

Chapter One

Mike Croft turned away from the crime scene and walked along the head of the gully towards the second stile. Beyond that, the path broadened out, allowing an avenue of sunlight to break through between the tall trees. He climbed over the stile, relieved to get out of the darkness and into the warmth of the early summer's day. The sudden heat on his back was enough to persuade him out of his jacket.

He held a large-scale OS map in his hand and referred to it now. Further along, the path apparently turned into a gated road leading back towards Honiton.

Which way had Jake Bowen come in? Mike wondered. The narrow road and rabbit path that Macey and Liz Corran had taken or this other road? And had the woman been alive when he brought her here?

Mike leaned heavily against the fence post next to the stile, facing into the sun. This last six months, he felt, he'd done nothing but live and breathe Jake Bowen, especially since he'd been seconded to the operation eight weeks ago, along with practically anyone who'd ever had dealings with the killer. Mike had found himself dragged over half the country, chasing one short-lived lead after another, finally fetching up here – the middle of nowhere and a long way from home.

'Penny for them?'

Mike turned with a slight smile. 'Not worth it, sir. I was trying to work out the last time I had a weekend off.'

Chief Superintendent Mark Peterson returned the smile. 'Probably about the same time I did,' he said. 'And it's not likely to be this weekend either.'

'No, I suppose not. I'd arranged for Maria to come down.'

'Ah. I'll tell our man to improve his timing.' He paused for a moment. 'Look, Mike, get your lady to come anyway. Unless something breaks fast, you'll be able to wangle a couple of hours free.'

'Thanks. I'll do that.'

Peterson leaned against the fence and gazed out, eyes squinting, into the sunny space between the trees.

'I've got someone walking in from the other end, looking for tyre tracks, anything out of the ordinary.'

'Doubt they'll find anything. Last two weeks have been too damned dry. I asked one of the locals,' Mike added by way of explanation.

'You been down there yet?' Peterson gestured towards the gully.

'Briefly. I came back up top, let the photographer and SOCO do their bit. There's enough bodies down there as it is.'

Peterson laughed gruffly at the unintended humour. 'We'd better get back and join them,' he said, 'they've just warned me the surgeon's on his way.'

A sound overhead made both men look up sharply. A squirrel, its tail flying out behind it, leapt between trees. Peterson laughed again. There was relief in the sound of it. 'You know, Mike. I'm not a man given to all that much imagination, but if, when we find this bugger, he's got hooves and a forked tip to his tail, I'm not going to be surprised.'

A shout from behind them in the gully told them that the police surgeon had arrived. Mike eased himself over the stile and they made their way back along the path. Peterson's comment had come as no surprise; everyone was as jumpy as hell. He glanced sideways. The man's rather round face, reddened by too much sun, had gained lines these last weeks. Peterson was a robust man, taller than Mike's six two and heavier, but the strain of the Bowen hunt was beginning to tell on him and recently he seemed to have shrunk in on himself.

Some fifteen years older than Mike, Peterson was a career copper who'd made it up through the ranks. His present title, Chief Super, was being phased out in one of the 'reforms' sweeping through the service and men like Peterson, who seemed to belong to another time, were finding it hard to make their way in the new order. Promoted sideways to head up 'Operation Final Frame' – Mike wondered who made these names up – this was likely to be the last thing Peterson would see through before he retired.

DI Mike Croft had grown to like and respect the man a great deal and knew it was an opinion largely shared by the rest of the team. Under other circumstances, Mike would have enjoyed working with this large, bluff man with the overgrown moustache. Under these circumstances, Mike wished himself anywhere but here.

It was not an easy scramble down into the gully. Tree roots reaching from the dry ground and hard, rutted furrows cut by the last heavy rains then dried by the summer heat threatened to undermine every step. The scene, when they reached bottom, was pretty much as Macey and Liz had viewed it. It looked, thought Mike, like a scene from a low-budget horror flick, but this was real. The woman's long hair was carefully combed out across the bed of flowers on which she lay, her hands folded prayerfully between her breasts, and a long, thin line of blood had flowed from the artery in her throat down across the flowers. White roses stained a rusty brown.

'Bled her like a bloody pig,' Peterson said.

Chapter Two

'Death confirmed at four thirty-five p.m., Friday 18 June. And before you ask, a quick estimate just from body temperature, ambient conditions and all that rot, I'd say she's been dead maybe four, five hours.'

'That would make time of death around midday.'

'No, that would make my rough estimate around midday. When was the body found?'

'Two fifteen, two twenty or thereabouts. The call came in at two thirty-seven. Mobile phones don't do so well around here. The pair who found her had to go back to the farm on the main road and call in on a land line.'

Peterson frowned. 'They claim to have received their tip-off at around one this afternoon. The call was made from a telephone box in Honiton.'

Mike had been looking more closely at the trail of blood. 'I'd have expected more spattering. More spread. The blood's run in just this one stream.'

The police surgeon looked impressed. 'I was coming to that. You're quite right, arterial blood usually spurts in all directions. Maybe our man was intent on not getting his clothes dirty. Maybe to keep to our timescale, he couldn't allow himself time to change.'

'So she was already dead when he brought her here?' Peterson asked.

'No, I didn't say that. What it probably means is that he reduced the pressure sufficiently for it not to spurt. My guess, and it's only a guess as yet, is he wanted the effect without getting himself covered.' He paused, his mouth curved with distaste. 'To put it bluntly, he drew off sufficient to lower the pressure before he even got her here. Then he arranged things neatly and finished the job.'

Mike felt sick. Murder he had dealt with many times, but Jake Bowen had the knack of going well beyond previous experience.

'Well, then, we've answered one question,' Peterson said harshly. 'Poor kid certainly didn't walk here.'

He turned away and Mike followed him back up onto the path.

'The Jacksons are letting us have use of their barn as an incident room. Just as well! We'd never get a mobile up those narrow lanes and I'm pulling in all the extra bodies they'll let me have, posting a twenty-four-hour, two-man patrol to keep the trophy hunters at bay.'

Mike nodded. 'I don't envy the night shift,' he commented. 'This hole's bleak enough in daylight.'

'What daylight?' Peterson gestured. 'It's all just bloody dead. Downright weird if you ask me.' He paused again as though not sure how to say what he had in mind. 'Do you believe in spirit of place, Mike? You know, you'll go somewhere and it'll feel wrong.' He went on without waiting for an answer. 'This place. I mean, it's like it's been waiting here, all this time, just for something like this to happen.'

He laughed, trying to dispel the notion.

'I've known places like that,' Mike said quietly. 'There was one I came across when I first worked in East Anglia. A place called the Greenway. It was only a pathway, with these damned great hedges either side of it, but there was always this feeling about it. Something that said we didn't belong there.'

Peterson smiled. 'It's getting to all of us, isn't it? We know so much about this man and yet the more we know, the further away he seems to get. Damn it, Mike, we even know the bugger's name. No wonder the bloody press are making us a laughing stock. Four deaths and he's pre-warned us about each one. And we're no bloody closer.'

Mike nodded in silent sympathy. It had all been said and he had nothing to add, but Peterson wasn't finished.

'It's the sort of thing you'd expect to see in some American slasher movie. You know, some place where crossing the county line actually means something, and with so much bloody space the states are like separate countries. But I mean, look at this. A goddamned wood in the middle of Dorset and we're chasing this psycho who even has the cheek to send us photo locations before he commits the crime.'

He reached into his pocket, withdrew copies of three photographs and held them out in front of Mike, who didn't bother to look.

'It could have been anywhere,' Mike said quietly. 'A few fallen trees and a bit of a bush. Nothing to set it aside from a thousand other places across the country, not until you see the real thing.'

Peterson shook his head and continued to regard the

pictures, comparing them to the actual scene. Then he shoved them back in his pocket. 'I know. You're right,' he said. 'Hindsight's a wonderful thing, but you think our bosses are going to look at it that way? Or the media? Or Joe Public? Damn it, Mike. One man and he's got most of the population locking themselves in after the *Six o'clock News* every night.'

He sighed, rubbed tired eyes with the heels of his hands, then straightened himself up. 'Get yourself back to Dorchester, find out how the interviews with our friends from the press are going. I'll see things are finished up here.'

Mike nodded. 'One thing's for certain,' he said wryly. 'Mr Ed Macey finally got his exclusive.'

Chapter Three

The murder in the woods near Honiton, just above the Jacksons' farm at Colwell Barton, had made the national evening news. At that point, no connection had been made between this and the three others attributed to Bowen, but, as had become typical, Jake Bowen himself had drawn public attention to his latest escapade.

The pictures of Liz and Macey standing in the woods surrounded by half-burnt candles appeared in two of the morning editions of the tabloids.

Liz found Macey staring at the front pages scattered over the top of his desk.

'You've seen them then?'

'What do you think?' He looked up at her, then pushed an office chair in her direction. 'Sit down before you fall down. Christ, you look bad!'

'Thanks a bunch. I didn't sleep, OK? You got a cigarette?'

'Thought you'd given up.'

He pushed the packet towards her. Liz was new to this game, a mere trainee. He wondered, looking at her pale face and red eyes, if she'd be changing her mind on a career in journalism. Most kids at her stage of the game were writing Local Notes on the village fête, not encountering dead bodies in remote woodland. Her hands trembled as she sparked up and she drew a deep, unsteady breath before managing a weak smile.

'I'll be OK,' she said.

'Sure you will. Sure you will. We've been summoned to another chat with Detective Inspector Michael Croft later this morning. Dumb shit probably wants to accuse me of taking these.' He gestured angrily at the tabloid pictures. 'God, Liz, but I wish I bloody had. I truly do.'

'You don't mean that.'

'Don't I? All my working life I've waited for something like this. It falls in my lap and I can't take advantage. There's no justice. No bloody justice at all.'

Liz said nothing; she was learning to take little notice of Macey's bluster. Instead, she pulled the pictures towards her, trying to be calm.

'He'd have to think you were some kind of cool shit to have taken these,' she said. 'Stood there with a dead body, set the camera on a timer and posed with that real shocked look on your fat face.'

She broke down then, covering her face with her cigarette-free hand and sobbing bitterly, still deep in shock.

'He was there, Macey. There in the woods watching us all the time. We could be dead by now, don't you understand that? You're going on about missing the chance of a lifetime and we could be fucking dead.'

Macey reached out and put what he hoped was a comforting hand on Liz's shoulder. She was right, he just didn't want to tell himself that. The two pictures that had been spread right across the front pages of the morning news showed the clearing in the gully shadowed by trees and slightly unfocused, as though to preserve some sense of decency. But clear enough and in the foreground, the shock and disbelief on their faces so plainly written, stood Liz and Macey.

The morning news was full of it. Maria Lucas had watched it on the television: the pictures of the latest Bowen outrage and the predictable responses from anyone and everyone who could wangle a little airtime.

Library pictures showed Chief Superintendent Peterson speaking at an earlier press call and Mike Croft, almost out of shot, looking as though he'd slept in his suit and had not shaved for at least a week.

It was, Maria mused, about the only time she got to see him these days. Brief glimpses caught as he sought to avoid the press photographers or the TV cameras. She knew from the odd times they had managed to talk that the strain of conducting this investigation so much in the public eye was becoming unbearable.

The phone rang. She picked it up on the second ring.

'Oh, good morning, John. Yes, I saw him. I guess this puts paid to our plans this weekend.'

She could hear John Tynan's smile. 'That's the penalty for being involved with a policeman, my dear. Seriously though, it's a nasty business.'

Maria sighed. 'Isn't it always? I was going to give you a call later anyway, see if you were free tonight.'

'Yes, I think so. What did you have in mind?'

'Essie,' Maria told him. 'Jo's still in the hospital, likely to stay there until this baby's born, and, as you know, Essie's still at my moma's place. I thought I'd give everyone a break and take her to see the latest Disney or something.'

'And you're not keen on facing it alone? No, certainly I'll come. I'd love to. Essie's a pleasure, though are you sure Disney isn't a bit tame for her? I thought space aliens with big guns were more up her street.'

Maria laughed. 'Probably, but as she's only five I think we might have problems getting her in. Anyway, I'll find out the times and give you a ring around lunch time. That's if I get a lunch time.'

'Heavy workload?'

'You wouldn't believe it. Prozac must be the in fix this season.' She glanced at the clock. 'OK, got to go, John. Catch you later.'

She rang off and began to get her notes in order. Maybe, she thought, if Mike was going to be tied up all weekend, she should offer to have Essie. Maria's sister, Jo, was expecting her second child and, with high blood pressure and oedema, was having something of a rough time. It would be a load off everyone's mind if Auntie Maria stepped into the breach.

Mike and Peterson watched the officers file out after the morning briefing. The barn which had been commandeered as their incident room was hardly ideal. No animals, but the place was still half-filled with hay bales and feed sacks piled against one wall. The flagstone floor struck cold even on the summer morning and Mike was glad that at least this was not happening in the middle of winter.

There was electricity in the barn, or rather there were two overhead lights. A generator was promised for later that morning to power essential equipment, and it had not yet been decided if this should be set up as a long-term incident room or just a temporary feature. That would depend on what was found at the crime scene, what witnesses came forward and on Jake Bowen's next move.

Two cats lounged in the patch of sunlight that poured through the open door. Eight thirty, but the last of the mist had evaporated and the day was already hot. The bright sunlight threw the rest of the barn into deep shadow and Mike turned the pin-board he was setting up towards the light to give himself a clearer view. He was pinning up pictures of the scene in the woods and of Jake Bowen's previous known victims. There were others, still unproven, filling a stack of files and untold disk space back at Honiton and elsewhere, but, Mike figured, to display that would take more than a pin-board and be a task too depressing to even attempt.

Peterson pulled out a chair, reversed it and sat down. He'd let Mike handle the morning briefing and assign the search teams and two local mobile units to carry out the door-to-door inquiries. Neighbours were well scattered, a few along the single track road, more placed well back along rutted lanes or accessible only on foot.

It was a task complicated by the number of visitors. The farm across the valley and a couple of others further along the road had been given over to the tourist trade.

Folk just there on holiday and intent on relaxing and enjoying themselves probably wouldn't notice the unusual if it got up and hit them in the face. Many would be in residence only at the ends of the day, not be around to see murders committed at noon. Add to this, as they'd found out the night before, that there were at least four well-established footpaths into the woods, with as many offshoots from each one. When Jake Bowen had chosen what looked like a public time and a public place, he'd certainly known exactly what he was about.

Peterson looked across to where Mike was pinning the photographs.

'Four murder victims,' he said, 'in five months.'

'That we know of.'

'Don't make life complicated, Mike. OK, four that we can prove. And not a bloody thing to connect them.'

'We can add the Norwich rapes,' Mike persisted, carefully aligning one of the photographs with the edge of the board. 'Three of them anyway, and the woman at Kennet in Wiltshire, Marion O'Donnel, all late last year. Whatever else he might be, our man's no slouch.'

Peterson got up, came across to where Mike was standing and began to sort through the notes and pictures lying on the table. It had been Mike Croft's involvement with a spate of violent attacks on women on his home patch of Norwich that had first brought him into contact with Jake Bowen. That had been at the tail-end of the previous year. Peterson himself had become involved in early February of this, when a young woman had been found brutally murdered in a Bristol park. With the turning of the year, Jake Bowen had moved west.

'You spoke to the two reporters last night,' Peterson said. 'First impressions?'

Mike thought about it. Ed Macey and Liz Corran's statements had been analysed at the morning's briefing. Peterson was after a personal response.

'The caller asked for Macey,' he commented. 'That's typical Bowen behaviour, pick on someone specific, someone local, someone who's likely to want to get involved.'

'Wouldn't that go for any reporter?'

'Maybe, but Macey's been working on provincials all his life.' Mike shrugged. 'Some people would like it that way, but I think not Edward Macey. He talked last night about looking for a break into the big time before it was too late.' He paused, pinned up an enlargement of the wound in the victim's throat. 'The young woman, Liz Corran, I think we can see her presence as incidental to Bowen's plans. I'm sure he wanted Macey as a witness and went to great lengths to get him there.'

'Which, betting on Bowen following his previous pattern, means he might well make contact again.'

'He might,' Mike agreed. 'The officers who inter-viewed Macey's associates say he's apparently in the habit of mouthing off in his local when he's had a few. Goes on about how he could have been working on one of the nationals if he'd had the right breaks or the right connections.'

'And that's just the thing Jake Bowen would be on the lookout for.' Peterson nodded. 'And asking round here if there'd been any strangers in the local pubs would get us laughed out of court. We're in the middle of the bloody tourist season.'

'Not quite.' Mike smiled wryly and went to fill the kettle from the tap on the wall. They hadn't asked, but had assumed that this was drinking water. At any rate, it tasted all right in tea. 'The real tourist season begins when the schools finish. That's the third week in July around here, so it's worth asking. We'll get a list of conflicting information a mile long, especially as Macey's "local" could be any one of three or four pubs, but I've got a couple of officers on to it.'

Peterson nodded. 'Have you spoken to Maria yet?'

'No. She was out when I called last night. I'll have another go mid-afternoon. She generally grabs ten minutes or so then.'

Peterson shook his head. 'I think my wife's forgotten who I am,' he said. Then, 'So what do we have? A woman caller. Asks for Ed Macey and gives him a map reference and a time and tells him that there'll be something useful waiting for him.'

'Yes. She sounded drunk, Macey said, and wouldn't answer any of his questions.'

Peterson took a copy of Macey's statement from the table, glancing through it. 'He mentions that she kept giggling and breaking off to confirm with another person that she'd got it right.' He dropped the statement back on the table. 'I mean, anyone else would have reckoned it to be a wind-up and put the phone down.'

'But not Macey. He *wanted* this to be real. The caller only had to mention Jake Bowen's name and he'd be there, on the line with the worm in his mouth.'

'I agree.' Peterson frowned. 'We know how thorough our man is. It's obvious he's talked to Macey or at the very least observed him.'

Mike shrugged. 'Macey is not what you'd call a quiet man,' he commented. 'My guess is, with a few pints inside him, you could sit way across the saloon bar and still not need to read lips to know what was on his mind.'

'So that leaves the woman. The call came in at one p.m. and we're assuming our victim had probably been dead for around an hour by then.' He paused and reached across to see to the kettle, which had just come up to the boil. 'So we have to ask ourselves, does Bowen have a friend or relative living in the area? Someone to make the call for him. Did he meet some woman in the pub and get her drunk, tell her it was some kind of a prank?' He dunked tea-bags in the mugs and then handed one to Mike. 'I don't like what you're thinking.'

Mike took the mug. 'Neither do I,' he said, 'but we both know Bowen's record. He's too thorough, too organized, to use someone he just picked up in a pub, unless he was very certain they'd not talk about it. A friend? Relative? Maybe. My bet is, though, whoever made that call is going to be Bowen's next kill.'

Chapter Four

Mike drove out to Dorchester to speak with Liz and Macey. He found Macey sitting in a side office behind a desk piled high with newspaper clippings and handwritten notes.

'All the stuff I have so far on Jake Bowen,' Macey told him. 'I've even got you in amongst that lot somewhere.'

'Oh?' Mike queried.

'Your work on the Norwich rapist,' Macey told him. 'Or should that be in the plural?'

Mike poked a cautious finger at the stacks of paper perched precariously on the edge of the desk. 'You've done your homework,' he commented.

'Some good it's been. I'm there, literally in the picture, and some bastard on the nationals gets all the credit for it. Didn't even have to do the work for it either.'

Mike found a free chair and sat down. 'You'll have them beating a path to your door and you know it. First impressions. The inside story from the man who saw it all.'

Macey snorted. 'Yeah, maybe.' He was reluctant to confirm what Mike had said, but he was feeling a whole lot better than he had done earlier in the day. Already the phones had been buzzing; big names wanting to get on the inside track. He looked sharply at Mike.

'So, what's your line this morning? Have you come

here to make sure I don't talk or to accuse me of taking those flaming pictures?'

Mike smiled. 'You watch too many bad films, Macey. No, I'm here because we think you may have had contact with the killer at some time, maybe the last week or ten days.'

'Contact? With the killer?' Macey's face turned purple and then pale. 'Now look here, Detective Inspector Croft, if you're accusing—'

'No one's accusing, so cut the outraged voice-of-the-people act.' Mike paused and rubbed a hand across tired eyes. He couldn't remember the last time he'd been anything but tired. 'Look, you might have talked to him in passing. Talked in front of him. Complained too loudly about not getting a piece of the action. Anything, as simple as that. Jake Bowen's got a peculiar sense of humour, that much we do know, and all it might take for him to involve you in his game could be the odd word in the wrong place at the wrong time.'

Macey's mind was working overtime. Random thoughts that had plagued him through a sleepless night now started falling into place.

'He asked for me by name,' Macey said. 'It could have been anyone, but he asked specifically for me.'

Mike sat forward suddenly. 'Now wait a minute. It was a woman who made that call.'

Macey shook himself. 'Sure,' he said. 'But it was a man who spoke to reception. It was only a woman on the line when it was put through to me.'

'A man,' Mike said heavily, 'and you didn't see fit to mention this in your statement?'

'I didn't know, not until this morning, when I started to ask around. Talk to the girl yourself. You'd better hurry, though. Once she starts putting two and two together and realizes she was chatting to a murderer, she'll be off like a flash. You mark my words.'

Mike wondered if Macey always talked in clichés.

'I'll be talking to her,' he said heavily, 'just as soon as I've done with you, Mr Macey. The fact that he didn't speak to you himself, that could be significant.'

'You mean I might have known the voice? Yes, I'd considered that. Look, I'll give it some thought.'

'You'll give it more than some,' Mike told him. 'I want to know. Anyone strange or anyone in one or other of your local watering holes who might have shown an unusual interest in you or what you have to say?'

'Aw, come on, Inspector. I work for a bloody newspaper. Look, knowing that – and, believe me, most of them do where I choose to drink – well, most people it takes in one of two ways. Either they shut up tight when I'm around or they won't bloody give over. It's all, "Oh, I've got a good story for you, mate," ' Macey mimicked. 'Or, "There's something going on at such and such a place you ought to be looking at." Then when they find out I'm a bloody photographer, they all want cheap rates on their kiddie portraits. It's like being a frigging doctor – no such thing as off duty. There's always someone got something suppurating they want you to take a look at.'

He pushed back his chair and got up, pacing the little space there was left in the room.

'I mean, what does this fellah look like?' He waved an impatient hand towards his stacks of paper. 'A good half-dozen descriptions you've got there and not one of them the same. He's got blond hair. He's got dyed black hair. He's clean-shaven when he hasn't got a beard or an occasional moustache. He's got blue eyes that might be brown and a Geordie accent according to some vicar in Berkshire who might be talking about the Lord God himself for all the reliability of it. You've got some forensic shrink that profiles him as a lorry-driving loner and a wannabe Doris Stokes that claims she's in contact with him on a higher plane. Fuck it, Inspector. You know the man's name. You think he might be from up north because you've got a couple of Jake Bowens up there you haven't been able to track through the voters' register and that's about it. Oh, I'm sorry, you know he kills people and likes to make artistic films about it. He probably even takes a starring role. And you can take a guess that he's going about his business under an assumed name.'

Mike opened his mouth to speak, his own anger and frustration beginning to break through, but Macey hadn't finished.

'I talk to a lot of people, Inspector Croft. You do in my game and a lot of people ask me a lot of daft questions about what I do.' He sat down again and reached across for a stack of papers. 'I'll tell you something for nothing. This guy's not going to hang around waiting for you to get a fix on him. He's mobile and he's smart and, you mark my words, he's done what he set out to do. He's long gone.'

Mike shook his head slowly. 'I think you're wrong,' he said. 'I've seen the way Jake Bowen works and he's

not finished yet. Those pictures, they were just the beginning. He caught you on film. Just one frozen moment,
but that won't be enough for Jake Bowen. He likes his
pictures live and moving or spectacularly dead. I'll make
a bet with you, Macey, he's already got an archive on
you that would make what you've got on him look like a
kids' dictionary put beside the *Encyclopaedia Britannica*.
You might hope he's left, but Jake Bowen makes feature-
length editions and so far all you've contributed are a
few stills.'

Mike had a swift word with both Liz and the receptionist
who had taken the call, but his patience was short and
he did not want to push it further. He normally saw
himself as calm and controlled – *too* controlled, Maria
was always telling him – but Macey had reached under
his skin and he had reacted.

Liz had little to add to her previous statement. She
was clearly still shaken and was chain-smoking cigarettes
in a non-smoking office as though to make up for the
weeks when she'd been trying to give them up.

'I'm OK, though,' she told him. 'Damned if this thing
is going to get to me.'

The receptionist had nothing useful to tell. 'An
ordinary voice,' she said. Not a local accent, but not one
that she could place either.

Mike made a note to get an officer sent out to take
a formal statement but held out little hope that it would
get them anywhere. Ordinary voice. That was just the

trouble with everything they knew about Jake Bowen. Much of it was so damned ordinary.

It was mid-afternoon before Mike managed to talk to Maria and suggest that she come down to see him that weekend.

'Oh, Lord, I'm sorry, Mike. I thought with all this business going on you'd be tied up and I've volunteered to have Essie.'

'Oh.' He knew it was inadequate, but it was all that he could manage. He tried again. 'There's no one else? I take it Jo's still in hospital?'

'I'm afraid so. Look, I'll ring Moma, see if I can come down on Sunday at least. Or,' she said tentatively, 'I could bring her with me?'

Mike hesitated. He was loath to bring a child to where Jake Bowen might be, even though he knew that was probably stupid, as Bowen could be just about anywhere. Rather hesitantly he explained this to Maria, half expecting her to laugh at him.

'I see what you're saying, Mike. OK. Look, I've not said for certain I'd be able to have Essie at the weekend. I'll try and sort something out and make it up to everyone another way. I'll drive down Friday night if you can book me in somewhere. It's going to be late, but at least we'll have the weekend together.'

'It's a long drive, love, and I can't promise I'll be there all the time.'

'I'll be fine. Anyway, I'm missing you.' She laughed

suddenly. 'Maybe I should bring John with me. Kind of family reunion.'

'Don't even think of it. Much as I'd love to spend some time with him, I need time alone with you more. I'll ring you tonight.'

He listened as she put the phone down before switching the mobile off and starting back towards Honiton, thinking about Maria. Having her say she missed him was precious. He'd known her almost two years now and found it impossible to imagine life without her, though it still amazed him that someone as beautiful could choose to be in love with him.

Mike carried her picture in his wallet. He had always thought that a rather sentimental thing to do, but now he found it comforting to be able to open it and see her smiling at him, head slightly to one side. Her smile raised dimples in the richness of perfect black skin and her dark eyes sparkled with mischief. She wore her hair close-cropped. Before Maria, Mike had always preferred hair to be long. But that was then. Now he viewed everything about her as perfect.

It would be good to see her at the weekend, even if only for the briefest of times.

Though the strain still showed itself around his eyes, Mike was actually smiling as he drove down into Honiton.

When Liz went to find him, Macey was still poring over his Jake Bowen archive. He'd spent the hours since Mike had left on the phone, returning calls, chatting to editors whose names he'd previously only read at the head of their columns. Macey was one of an increasingly rare breed. He might work for the *Dorchester Herald* as a photographer, but he'd done his time as a journalist and that made him a one-man band, ready and eager to produce the goods for whoever wanted to pay.

He'd agreed to a couple of interviews, but what he really wanted was the by-line and finally he'd forced tentative agreements from a couple of tabloid editors. Find a new angle and we'll publish. Macey's rational side told him that such verbal contracts weren't worth the proverbial paper they were written on, but he didn't care. This was going to be it and it was Mike Croft who had given him the germ of an idea. The angle. If Jake Bowen hadn't finished yet with Macey, well maybe he could use it to his advantage. A genuine inside story with Macey as the leading man.

And the *Herald* wanted their share of the glory too. The editor was determined that Macey should not sell them short and, going back over his notes, he thought he had just the thing to satisfy.

'Charlie Morrow,' he announced as Liz came through the door.

'Charlie who?'

'Morrow. He put two and two together about Jake being the killer movie-maker he was after. Specialist stuff. Very select audience. Used the one-shot casting principle.'

'The what? Macey, what the hell are you on about?'

'His actors. You get to feature in a Jake Bowen special, it's likely to be your one and only chance of stardom. You burn bright, but by God you have a short career.'

'You're talking the snuff movies this guy is supposed to have made?'

'No supposed about it, Liz. They're real enough and they're still out there, getting more valuable by the frigging day. This guy, Morrow. He was a DCI from what I remember. Led a raid on one of Bowen's studios and got himself blown up for his trouble.'

'And?' Liz queried.

'You and I are going to talk to him. See how he's getting along.' He grinned at her. 'Editor says we need a good story for the local rag, something the big boys haven't covered, and my feeling is that Charlie Morrow could be it.'

Liz frowned. 'If it's such a good story, how come no one else has touched it?'

'Because up until about a month ago he was still in hospital, specialist burns unit, and they weren't about to let hordes of journos clutter up their waiting room. Anyway, after all the initial fuss was over and he failed to die from his injuries, the story kind of faded out.'

'And you think you can revive it?'

'Sure I can. Few phone calls – well, actually every bloody nursing home in Wiltshire or near enough – and I've found him.'

'And they told you he was there, just like that?'

'Well, no, not just like that. I called and asked to speak to him. Number five and I struck lucky. They put the call through to his room.'

'And he talked to you?' Liz was caught between outrage and astonishment.

'Well . . .'

'He told you where to go. Words that start with F and end with off by any chance?'

Macey laughed. 'That was his first reaction, but I talked him round. Told him who I was, mentioned Jake Bowen's name.'

'God, Macey, I'd think that was the last thing he'd want to hear.'

'Ah.' Macey tapped gently on the side of his several-times-broken nose. 'That's where you're wrong. Ex-DCI Charlie Morrow is very interested in Jakey boy's latest escapade.'

'Jakey boy! Christ, you make me sick sometimes.' She shook her head. 'I still can't believe he's agreed to see you.' She looked more shrewdly at Macey. 'He hasn't agreed, though, has he? *Has he?* This is all just so much pie.'

Macey pushed himself to his feet with an air of injured importance. 'Not yet, my girl, but he will. You just mark my words.'

Chapter Five

Friday morning was as hot as ever, even at eight o'clock, when Mike set out from Honiton. He was lodging in a cramped room above a pub. The accommodation was basic but adequate, and Mike was quite content with it. All in all, it was probably more comfortable than his flat in Norwich, a one-bedroomed affair he had rented half-furnished and to which he had added very little in the two years he had been there.

He was on his way to see Max Harriman. Harriman had been a close friend of Jake when the two of them were growing up and he'd maintained contact with him in a distant way ever since. He had regarded Jake as something of a hero, mimicking his actions, though he lacked Jake's innate caution and sense of purpose. He had finally been arrested when his imitation of Jake had gone too far. He had raped and then killed in December of the previous year.

Harriman was still on remand awaiting final psychiatric assessment before going to trial, the wheels of the judiciary moving as slowly as ever. He was presently being held in a secure psychiatric unit and Mike had been seeing him several times a month since then, sometimes at Harriman's instigation and sometimes his own.

Harriman should have been their key to Jake. It was because of him that they knew Jake's real name and anything about his background, but, Mike reflected as he drove out on this latest visit, that still didn't amount to a great deal. Harriman had played them like an expert over these last months and many times Mike had felt like threatening to withdraw his visits, which seemed to lead to nothing but frustration and only fed Harriman's sense of self-importance. His superiors, though, had said he must carry on. Mike had been the arresting officer and, for whatever reason, Harriman had chosen him to be the one he'd talk to. From time to time he'd let slip some little detail; some fragmentary clue to the way Jake thought or the way he might behave. It was enough to make them consider cultivation of Max Harriman worthwhile.

Beside Mike on the passenger seat lay a large folder. Inside were copies of the cuttings books Max had kept over the years, with material from local papers, from the nationals, even from the occasional glossy magazine. Max must have spent a fortune on his news collection. Not all of the articles concerned Jake and Max; it was an eclectic mix. Max had taken care to record noteworthy incidents in the lives of anyone he had once known and grown up with: the weddings of one-time friends; births of their children if they appeared in the paper; even the small achievements of those children, such as the time one had won first prize in a dance competition or another been a May Queen's attendant at the local fête.

Everyone mentioned in Max's books had been traced, interviewed, tagged and quietly turned inside-out, on the off-chance Jake Bowen might still be known to them.

Macey had been wrong in what he'd said the day before. They knew a great deal about Jake Bowen: the young man growing up in what had been a pit village just outside York; the young man who had shown such promise at school – when he could be bothered to attend. They knew about the teacher Ian Wright who'd borrowed the super eight cine camera on Max and Jake's behalf and helped them make a film that had won a prize in a national competition, and, unknowingly, set Jake on a career that would make him the most hunted and probably the most feared man in Britain.

Jake Bowen had been just fifteen years old then and his picture, with Max, in the local paper was the last image they could be certain they had of him.

They knew that Jacob Alastair Bowen had been born on 9 November 1959 to Millie and Alastair Bowen. He was an only child, though Millie had suffered two miscarriages in previous years. Jake Bowen had grown up in the next street to Max Harriman. There were rows and rows of terraced, back-to-back houses with quiet roads between where the kids had played. The Bowens had a proper bathroom added to their home in 1964 and downstairs extension at the back. The Harrimans had beaten them to it by a year and been the first in their street to have a pink suite.

Harriman's reminiscences had been full of details like this.

Jake had gone to the local school, built originally as a Victorian Board School a few streets away. It still had the words carved above the doors denoting separate entrances for girls and boys. Mike had visited the school about a month before and it was still a Victorian Board School, for all that the staff had dressed it up inside, making the place more bright and cheerful than its founders could ever have intended. The holes in the tarmac of the school yard, Mike thought, were probably the same ones that Jake Bowen had fallen over, splashed in when it rained and played marbles in all those years before.

It was ordinary, recognizable. Mike himself had grown up in similar surroundings, geographically about a hundred miles south but in look and spirit very little different.

Police officers had converged on the little community over the past months, ostensibly mapping Max Harriman's career, but really more intent on tracking Jake. Mike knew that it would be only a matter of time before Max's connections with Jake Bowen came out, then the few details the police knew but the press and public did not would be splashed across every front page in the country. He could just visualize the headlines, the glaring spotlight trained on this small community when it finally became known that not one murderer but two had emerged from its quiet streets.

It was a two-hour drive to the prison even using the motorway and another half-hour dealing with the bureaucracy of the visit. Mike sat behind the wooden table in the bare room where it and two chairs were the only furnishings and laid out the cassette recorder he used during these interviews and the photocopied cuttings books.

The copies had been spiral-bound for ease of handling. Max Harriman's original books had been sugar-paper scrapbooks, of the sort that could be bought in any stationer's or post office. Stapled together and bound in stiff card. Harriman had made them more robust by covering the outside in sticky-back plastic.

The originals had been stashed away as evidence, but Max had been given a copy of each one in the hope that it would prompt him to make further disclosures. In practice Max spent more time bemoaning the loss of his originals than he did adding to their information. He would complain from the moment Mike came through the door, as he did today.

'You haven't brought my books. I told you, I wanted my books.'

'Good morning to you, Max. Sit down.'

Harriman sat down and shoved Mike's spiral-bound books away from him as though he found them distasteful.

'I told you, I don't say anything until I've got my books.'

'They're evidence, Max. You know that.'

'You've got copies. Use those as evidence.'

Mike didn't bother to reply this time. Instead he opened one of the books at a page he had previously marked and turned it so that Max could see.

'Last time I came to see you, we talked about Jake's parents.'

'No, Inspector, *you* talked about Jake's parents, I just listened. I told you, I can't do it without my books.'

'What happened to them, Max? Where did Jake's parents go to? We've got this one picture and nothing after that.' He leaned forward to see better and read the caption. ' "New lay preacher, Mr Alastair Bowen, at St Bartolph's Parish Church." ' He looked expectantly at Max, who said nothing. 'It's an odd thing for you to have saved, Max. A little clipping from a church magazine. Especially as neither you nor Jake could have been more than seven when it happened.'

Max glanced at him, then at the picture. 'It isn't mine,' he said.

'It was in your book.' Mike frowned. 'It's a funny thing, though, it was in one of the later books if I remember.' He flipped the cover over to check. 'Yes, I thought so. You must have added it later and not had room in the original book, so you put it in here. Five years ago, Max. What happened five years ago that you suddenly acquired this?'

'It isn't mine. I told you.'

'Then whose is it, Max? Are you suggesting that I made it up? Stuck it in a book and copied it just to fool you?'

Harriman gave Mike an almost pitying look. This was a routine they had repeated many times. Max sometimes even refused to acknowledge that the copies of the cuttings books bore any resemblance to the originals or had anything to do with him.

'If it were in my book I could tell you about it,' Max told him. 'That thing, it isn't mine.'

Mike shook his head thoughtfully. 'I can't let you have the originals, Max, you know that.'

'Why not? You've got copies. Lots of copies.'

'So you agree this is a copy of your book? If it's a

copy and you recognize that it's a copy, why can't you tell me about this clipping?'

Max sighed and leaned back in his chair, gazing up at the ceiling. Mike had learned over the course of many such sessions that the best thing he could do now was carry on, continue to talk, allow his conjectures to become wilder and wilder until Max was finally provoked enough to contradict him.

He pressed on. 'So what happened, Max? We know that the Bowens moved to York when Jake was twenty-one and that Jake went with them. We know that Jake was working in a printer's, that he was a plate maker. Very good, from what I'm told. We've traced them on the voters' register until 1982, when Jake would have been twenty-three, and then they drop out of sight. Now why was that?'

He sat forward, turning the book towards him. 'Where did the Bowens go to?' He let the silence sit for a little, then, as though thinking out loud, he said, 'It's strange, though. Alastair Bowen was a keen churchgoer all his life. Avid, you might say. Sang in the choir as a boy, joined an evangelical chapel as a young man and was a lay preacher at St Bartolph's right up until a month before they moved to York.'

'So?'

It was the first positive response of the morning, so Mike treated it with care. 'Well, doesn't it strike you as a little odd? I mean, we've absolutely no record even of church attendance in York. And I know, because I've talked to the minister who had the living at the time, that Alastair left the church quite suddenly. From being a mainstay of church activities to nothing, literally overnight, doesn't that strike you as strange, Max? Even a *little* strange?'

Max Harriman was sitting very still, his focus having switched from the ceiling to the wall behind Mike.

'And there's another thing. The minister from St Bartolph's said it was as though Alastair Bowen was afraid of something. Ashamed and afraid. That suddenly he wouldn't even speak to anyone from the church. Wouldn't let them into his house or take their calls when they phoned. Odd behaviour, don't you think? And I have to ask myself, Max, what was he afraid of? If the minister was right and he was ashamed of something, what do you suppose that could have been?'

Max blinked rapidly, as though awakening to Mike's presence again. 'He was a stupid man,' he said. 'Never understood.'

'Understood? Understood what?'

'Why – ' Max laughed and looked at Mike disbelievingly – 'Jake, of course. What Jake did, what he was, was beyond anything their small minds could understand.'

'Jake was special, then?' Mike pressed on, keeping his voice level and noncommittal, though he sensed they might be on the verge of something important.

'You know Jake was special. He always was, always will be to those of us who understand. Who have the vision to see beyond the act and look to the purpose.'

'And what purpose would that be?'

Max smiled at him, two bright spots of colour burning in an otherwise pale face, and his hands moved excitedly as though turning invisible pages to search for the right entry in the book.

'What happened to Jake's parents, Max?' Mike asked, hardly daring to raise his voice above the softest whisper. 'And Jake, where did Jake go to? Where did he go to next?'

Max's hands stopped moving abruptly, as though he had suddenly realized that the pages he was turning were unreal. What he was searching for wasn't there. 'I can't tell you without my books,' he said. Then he got to his feet, pushing the chair back so that it scraped loudly across the floor. 'I want to go now. I have nothing more to say. I want to go.'

It would be useless to press him further. Max could sit in stubborn silence for hours at a time once he'd set his mind against speaking. Mike watched the guard escort Max away and sat quietly, trying to assimilate what had and had not been said. He had come here today quite convinced that Jake Bowen had murdered his parents and had hoped to get some kind of confirmation from Max. Now, unaccountably, he was not so sure. What he had said to Max about having spoken to the old incumbent of St Bartolph's Church was a lie. The old minister had been dead and gone at least a dozen years. It had been guesswork on Mike's part, built on the slight evidence that Alastair Bowen had resigned from his position as lay preacher, but it looked as though he'd hit a target not so far from the truth.

Mike flipped open one of the other books. If the clippings held any clues, then Jake was already at least involved in the sex industry by then. Max's clippings recorded raids, in 1983, on two sex shops in the Bradford area, and another one, curiously, in Cardiff, where a quantity of magazines had been seized.

The evidence had long since been used to prosecute and would then have been destroyed, but from police records most were S&M mags of a particularly violent type. The report also stated that the pictures were very graphic, extremely realistic in their evocation of torture and of pain, and were taken by an obvious professional. It seemed that Jake Bowen knew his business even then.

Mike gathered his paperwork together and removed the tape from the machine. He glanced up as one of the guards who had escorted Max back to his cell came in.

'I hoped I'd catch you,' he said. 'Harriman got very excited when we were taking him back, wanted me to come and tell you something.'

'What was it?'

'Well, it's a bit odd really. He said to tell you that Jake sent him the picture five years ago and that you were right, he didn't have room for it in his proper book. Then he said I'd also got to tell you that his mother was a whore and the day she died was the only time he ever saw her smile.'

Mike got back into the car and turned on the radio. Peterson had held yet another press conference earlier that morning and details were given in brief on the lunch-time news, which Mike caught the tail-end of. Peterson was saying that he recognized the need for media exposure, that he realized public feelings were running high, and once again he appealed for help. Mike winced, knowing how Peterson really felt about all the media involvement, how much of a struggle it had been to keep anything under wraps.

Mike flicked the radio off and dialled the incident room number on his mobile phone. 'I'm on my way back,' he said when Peterson came on the line. 'I just heard you on the radio.'

Peterson snorted. 'Total farce,' he said. 'But you have to make the right noises. Anyway, we've got a development. I'm not going to say much over the air, but we know who she is. And she's been missing close on twelve weeks.'

'How?'

'Got lucky with a missing person's report. We're trying to locate kin. I'll fill you in when you get back. But the big question is, where the hell's she been all this time?'

Chapter Six

Mike had arrived in Lyme Regis at ten o'clock on the Saturday morning to find that Maria had already left for the beach. Their hopes of a romantic weekend had been dashed the night before. Her mother had called her literally as she had been about to leave with the news that Jo had gone into labour. She had to go to her, as Jo's husband, a sales rep, had been notified but would not be able to make it home for hours. Please could Maria help out?

She had called Mike immediately but had been unable to reach him. Undecided, the best she could manage was to leave a message telling him that she would be coming down but bringing Essie.

'They left about an hour ago,' the woman at the boarding house told him. 'The little girl was so keen to get to the beach.'

Maria had left instructions as to where they were likely to be and Mike went to see if he could find them.

He wasn't dressed for the beach but for the interview with the bereaved relatives he knew he would be meeting at some point that day. The girl in the woods had been called Julia. Julia Norman. Her parents, after weeks of anxiety, had finally been persuaded to spend a few days away with friends somewhere in the Midlands and it had taken time to track them down.

Julia had been a fine arts student. She had walked away from her course and the house she shared with four others without so much as a goodbye, taking only some clothes and the box containing most of her art equipment. That had been almost twelve weeks before and was the last anyone saw of her.

Anyone except Jake Bowen.

Mike loosened his tie and slung his jacket over his shoulder. He felt conspicuously overdressed among the shorts and T-shirts of the holiday-makers. He walked down the steep hill from the boarding house and cut through a shaded alleyway towards the beach. Maria had said they would be on the short stretch of sand close to the breakwater, looking out towards the Cobb. He strolled along the seafront, enjoying the bright sunlight and the blueness of the water, looking ahead and scanning the crowd for them.

It was Essie who saw him first. He heard her shouting his name.

'Uncle Mike, Uncle Mike! We're over here, Uncle Mike!'

Mike grinned and waved at the small figure in the red swimsuit. Her braided hair decorated with blue and yellow beads swung about her face as she leapt up and down trying to attract his attention. Water, sparkling like diamonds, splashed all around.

Mike strode across the stretch of sandy beach, picking his way between the sandcastles and sunbathers. Essie ran to him, arms outstretched. He hoisted her up, almost losing his jacket in the process, and her wet arms and plump sandy legs locked around his body.

'I love you, Uncle Mike.'

Mike cuddled the child close, inhaling the warm sunshine scent of her skin. It was a long time since his son Stevie had been this age and he had held him like this.

'I love you too, sweetheart,' he told her, looking over her head at Maria, who was walking up the beach towards him. She looked spectacular, he thought. Blue denim cut-offs and a white shirt open at the neck and tied below her breasts.

'Hi. I'd forgotten what you looked like.' Smiling, she kissed him, then looked with mild disapproval at his suit and tie. 'You're not dressed for making sandcastles, Uncle Mike.'

'I know, but I'm sure I'll manage.' He set Essie down and watched as she scampered back into the sea, aware of the damp patches on his shirt from wet, sandy limbs.

'You're likely to be called in?'

'They've identified the murdered girl. We finally managed to contact her parents late last night and they're expected back in Exeter this morning. Peterson's going to give me a call when they've made the formal identification. I'm really sorry, love, but I don't know how long I'm going to be.'

Maria slipped an arm through his and kissed him again. 'I knew it would probably be like that,' she said. 'Don't worry, we'll be just fine. Exeter, you say. She was a local girl then?'

Mike nodded. 'Born and brought up in Exeter. Studied at art college there, even lived in a shared house not two miles from her parents' home. Quiet and rather shy, according to her teachers. Then suddenly she breaks the pattern and takes off without a word.'

'Maybe no one knew her as well as they thought?'

'Maybe.' Mike sighed. He was dreading meeting the parents. 'Anyway,' he went on, 'I've got a while with you, and I can't tell you how good it is to see you.'

Mike had a little over an hour with Maria and Essie before the inevitable call came through. As brief a time as it was, it helped get his mind back into gear and his life back into perspective. As he allowed himself to relax and play with Essie and chat with Maria, he realized just how much tension had built up over the previous weeks and how heavily Jake Bowen weighed upon his mind.

Peterson's call, when it came, was brief and to the point. The parents had identified Julia and were insisting on seeing where the body had been found. Mike was to meet them at the crime scene with Peterson.

Mike frowned as he slipped the mobile phone into his pocket and told Maria he had to go.

'Is that unusual?' she asked. 'For people to want to see the place?'

'It happens, though usually later rather than immediately, but you can never tell what a bereaved family are going to do.'

He hugged Essie goodbye, getting wet again. He slipped his jacket on over the sand stains on his shirt and kissed Maria, promising he'd see them later, then walked back to find his car.

What had possessed a girl like Julia Norman to disappear as suddenly as she had and make no attempt to contact anyone? Or had she been unable to do so?

Twelve weeks of captivity was an awesome thing to contemplate. Mike wondered just how soon into that time she had known that she was going to die.

Mike was first to arrive back at the incident room in Colwell Barton. He spent the waiting time taking down the pin-board covered with the pictures of the dead girl and hiding it behind the hay bales in the corner, then tidying any other evidence out of sight. He heard the car pull up on the gravel outside only a few minutes later.

The Normans were middle-aged, a little older than Mike would have anticipated. He stood stiffly, shoulders squared as though to attention, his gaze deliberately concentrated on whoever might be speaking, while Mrs Norman could hardly bear to meet anyone's eyes.

Peterson made the introductions.

'I really am terribly sorry,' Mike found himself saying, hating himself for the meaninglessness of such platitudes but at a loss as to what else he might do.

Mr Norman nodded briefly and his wife murmured something that might have been thanks.

'You'll want to be getting on with this,' Peterson said brusquely. He'd spent time with them already and realized that sympathy at this stage was more than either of them could take. 'Mike, if you'd maybe lead the way. The going's a bit rough, I'm afraid,' he added, glancing down at Mrs Norman's summer sandals.

'If we could just go.'

Peterson glanced across at Mr Norman. 'Of course,' he said. 'Mike, would you . . .'

Mike led them along the narrow rabbit path and across the stile into the first patch of oakwood before they reached the Forestry Commission land. It was hot and still, silent but for the song of birds and their footsteps, half muffled by the grass. Peterson followed directly behind Mike after the first stile, leaving Mr Norman to help his wife. Her skirt and heeled sandals made it awkward for her to climb and Peterson had no wish to make her feel uncomfortable by having him watch her struggle.

Mike paused as they reached the second stile. 'It's just through here,' he said quietly. 'Are you certain you want to do this, Mr Norman? Mrs Norman?'

It was Julia's mother who answered, with surprising firmness. 'I need to see it,' she said. 'I won't believe it till I've seen the place.'

Reluctantly Mike led them on.

The gully was steep even for those in flat shoes but Mrs Norman would allow no one other than her husband to help. She laddered her tights and scratched her legs on the exposed tree roots, but she made it down.

The place where Julia's body had lain was still cordoned off, the yellow plastic of the tape seeming to glow in the semi-dark. Mrs Norman stood as close to the cordon as she could and stared at the rough altar of branches and now wilted flowers on which her daughter had died. Her gaze took in the dozens of tiny candles, burned down to mere stumps, that decorated the branches of the trees and travelled upwards to the dark canopy of leaves blocking the sunlight overhead. Then she let out a little cry before covering her mouth tightly with both hands.

'Are you all right, Mrs Norman?'

She nodded, hands still tight over her mouth as though she wanted to be sick. Her husband circled his arms around her and pulled her close.

'It's the same place, isn't it?' She pulled away enough so that she could look up into his face.

He nodded. 'Yes, I think it is.'

'The same place?' Peterson was questioning. 'Same place as what? You've seen this before, Mr Norman?'

'It's in a painting,' he said slowly, his voice thick with tears. 'At Christmas, Julia gave us a painting. One of hers. It was beautifully done, but it was not like her usual work.'

'A painting of this place?'

'Yes. This place. We knew it would be, that's why we had to come. We knew when you told us where she died. The flowers and the candles and all the things you told us, we had to come and be sure.'

'This painting,' Mike asked, 'it was more than just a landscape?'

'Oh, yes,' the father said softly. 'It was more than just a landscape. There was a woman lying on a bed of flowers. Lilies and white roses all painted so clearly you could tell what every one was meant to be. All stained with blood.'

Chapter Seven

Sunday morning brought a surprise in the shape of a phone call from Charlie Morrow. He and Mike had spoken during the earlier investigation and Mike had visited him several times while he had been in hospital receiving treatment for the severe burns he had suffered. He'd had a call from a couple of reporters, he told Mike. They'd done a good job of tracking him down and wanted to do a feature article on him.

'My first reaction was to say no, but I've been thinking about it and it might do some good. You've not exactly been getting sympathetic coverage.'

Mike laughed. 'No, it's been more like, why don't those useless coppers get off their backsides and get their collective fingers out. Seriously, though, do you feel up to joining the media circus?'

'I feel well enough to be bored out of my brain and very left out,' Charlie told him. 'I've been lying on my bloody back in hospital for months. No television in case it upsets me and no one willing to tell me a damned thing. I learned more interrogating Macey on the phone for ten minutes than I've pieced together in the past six months. Seriously, Mike, it's been the most frustrating time of my life.'

Mike sympathized and promised that he'd try to get to see him. He still wasn't used to the slight slur in

Charlie Morrow's voice when he spoke. The burns to the right side of his face had tightened the skin and scarred his upper lip badly enough to have necessitated grafts.

'I've had a lot of time doing nothing but think and there has to be something I can help on.'

'If I could offer you anything, Charlie, then you know I would. Lord knows we need the extra brain-power, but while you're officially on the sick . . .'

There was silence for a moment at the other end of the line. The truth was that it would be a long time, if at all, before Charlie Morrow returned to full duty.

'Charlie, I'm sorry. I really am.'

'Yes, I know. I know. But it rankles, Mike. I figure I owe that bastard one.'

Mike returned to Lyme to spend some time with Maria. They walked at Essie's pace along the shoreline out towards the headland jutting like a rocky finger into the sea. It was rough going over stones and heavy boulders, especially as Essie insisted on taking the hardest way across and shouting for Uncle Mike to look at every fossil that she found embedded in the rocks. Finally, they paused at a spot where the boulders gave way to flat rock, covered with weeds and broken by shallow pools full of shrimp and tiny fish. Essie was delighted, dipping her hands into the warm water, trying to catch the darting fish or sorting among the pebbles for the fossils that Mike had shown her how to identify.

The adults took the time to talk – a conversation interrupted every few minutes by another of Essie's finds, but still much more than they had enjoyed for many weeks.

Jo had given birth to a baby boy the night before and Maria looked forward to seeing the new addition to their family.

'You ever thought about having children?' Mike asked, surprised that he had never asked before.

Maria laughed. 'Are you proposing something?'

'Maybe. I don't really know. Sometimes I think, yes, I want to settle down again. Have kids before it's too late and I get too cynical or just too old.'

'Poor heading-for-middle-age man that you are.'

'Exactly that,' he said with a grin. 'Other times I think of Stevie, of how it felt when I lost him, and I know that I'm afraid of it happening again. Of having something as precious as a child and losing it.'

Maria reached for his hand and squeezed it tightly. She was about to speak when Mike stood up abruptly, turning to face the cliff and shading his eyes against the sun.

'What is it?'

'I thought I saw something. A flash of light, like something reflecting off a lense.'

Maria shrugged. 'Probably twitchers. There must be a ton of bird life up on the cliff.'

'I suppose you're right,' Mike said, but he continued to scan the clifftop, looking for the source of that elusive flash of light.

Maria touched his cheek, turning his face towards her. 'You're really spooked by all this, aren't you?'

'Anyone would be.'

'Of course they would, but, Mike, you've got to let up a bit or I'm going to be seeing you professionally.'

Mike tried hard to make light of it. 'I didn't think the rules allowed that,' he said.

Maria half smiled in return, but her eyes were worried. 'I'll have to bend the rules, then,' she said.

Chapter Eight

At the briefing in Honiton on the Monday morning Peterson unveiled the painting Julia Norman had given to her parents. He set it on a table leaning against the wall.

It was stunningly beautiful, Mike thought. A large canvas, some three feet tall by two across, the towering pine trees almost black against a glimpse of pale sky, with broken shafts of sunlight filtering through the branches, bleaching the colour from the ground.

The woman seemed to be at one with the scene. There was nothing anomalous about the figure lying prone upon a bed of flowers. The entire painting had a magical quality that allowed anything to happen within its frame.

Mike bent to look more closely at the figure. It was undoubtedly a self-portrait, with Julia's auburn hair and pale skin, her full lips curving in a slight smile. She looked as though she could have been dreaming.

Peterson had pictures of the crime scene, blown up to the same size and pinned to the wall beside the painting. He'd had them taken from as close to the same angle as he could get and it was obviously the same place, down to the details of the fallen trees and the light filtering onto the forest floor.

He turned towards those assembled.

'Your thoughts, please,' he said.

'She must have been there.'

'Maybe, or she could have painted from photographs.'

'So, did she take the pictures or did Jake Bowen?'

'It was a gift to her parents, sir?'

Peterson nodded.

'Well, it seems a bit of an odd thing to give your mum and dad. A nude self-portrait, I mean.'

'They thought it strange,' Peterson acknowledged. 'They said it was not like her usual stuff.'

'Have you seen any of her other work?' someone asked.

Peterson nodded. 'A couple of pictures they had at home. Most of it's still at the college and back at the house she shared. I'm having Mike collect it later this morning, but from what I've seen a lot of her work was semi-abstract stuff she was doing for her degree project. This is definitely not typical.'

'So why did she paint it?'

Mike took a few steps back, standing so that he could see both the painting and the photos of the crime scene from the same angle.

'It's summertime,' he said.

Peterson looked blank for a moment and then realized what Mike had said.

'And I'd say early summer,' he added. 'The greenness of it and just the general look. She either painted it last summer, in which case they'd probably have seen it at home – a canvas this size is not exactly an easy thing to hide – or she did it after she moved out in the autumn from pictures or sketches made earlier.'

'Her parents have no recollection of her coming here,' Peterson said thoughtfully. 'But, as you say, if she took the pictures herself or made working sketches, she must have come to the site well before her course began in October. She was only in her first year at the college. I've had a list made up of friends and associates, Mike, I'll leave you to go through it with the parents and identify those who are pre-college, so we can do a follow-up. Conningsby and Pierce, when the rest of her artwork gets here, see if she sketched this place or anything like it.'

'And we should look out for portraits,' Mike added. He indicated the painting. 'She obviously had some skill in that direction.'

'You think she might have drawn Bowen?'

Mike shrugged. 'We should be so lucky. It's possible. Anything's possible.'

'What if Bowen took the pictures? If she did the painting from those?'

'She could have got her reference material from anywhere,' someone else put in.

'But if Bowen did provide it, then it points to him coming here a full year ago. Maybe he took a holiday?'

'So, check all the local holiday properties for June and July.'

There was a general groan from those assembled.

'I know, I know. There must be tens of properties and hundreds of visitors, plus all the B&Bs and camp sites. Look, break it down. Start with those closest. Christ, I don't need to tell you how to do your jobs.'

He broke off as the phone rang. Mike picked it up.

'The front desk have got your wife on the line,' he said.

Peterson's usual beat was Bristol. He lived at Somerton with his wife, his two daughters having left home, one for university, the other married with three young children of her own. Jenny, the youngest, was there with her children when he and Mike arrived at his home an hour later and his wife met them at the door.

'Jenny's terribly upset,' his wife told him. 'I know I should have called the locals, but well, when you see the pictures, you'll know. It's got to be something to do with what you're working on.'

Peterson's daughter and three grandchildren were waiting in the kitchen. Only the oldest child, who was seven, seemed to have any comprehension of what was going on. She stood beside her mother's chair, clinging to her arm, while the other two played with Lego on the floor, arguing between themselves.

'Oh, Dad!' Jenny got to her feet and almost collapsed into her father's arms. 'I've been trying to get hold of Roger but he's out on site somewhere and his mobile's not switched on.'

'Did you tell them what was wrong? At Roger's work, I mean?'

She shook her head. 'No. Just that there was something urgent. He'll probably think one of the kids is ill, but I've left word that I'll be here. I'm not going back home, Dad, I'm not.'

Peterson held her tightly and then led her through to

the living room, while his wife took charge of the children. Mike followed.

'Sit down, Jen,' Peterson said.

She did as she was told. 'They're in there,' she said, pointing to a plastic freezer bag sitting on the table. 'I opened the envelope, obviously, and I looked inside, but as soon as I realized what it was I tried not to handle it too much. I just shoved everything in the bag and drove over here.' She smiled weakly. 'The way I was driving it's a wonder I didn't get arrested.'

'Never a policeman around when there should be.' Peterson returned the smile, then reached for the plastic bag and carefully emptied the contents onto the coffee table.

'These came with the normal post this morning?' Jenny nodded. 'This, a postcard from a friend on holiday and the phone bill.'

With the eraser end of a pencil, Peterson moved the six pictures around, spreading them out on the table. Three of the images seemed innocent enough: the children playing in the garden at their home, one on the swing, the others on the climbing frame; a bright summer afternoon, blue-skied and filled with sunshine. But the everyday images had been scanned into a computer and subtly changed so that at first it was not clear that there was anything wrong. You had to look closely to see the ligature around the neck of the youngest; the empty, bloody sockets of the oldest's eyes; the missing hand . . .

Peterson stood up abruptly and crossed the room, standing by the window and staring unseeing at the world outside. Jenny got up and joined him, clinging to his arm as her own child had done earlier to hers and hiding her face against his chest.

Quietly, Mike took plastic gloves and an envelope from the pocket of his jacket and gathered the pictures together, opening the envelope and hiding them inside.

Macey had been a little surprised when Charlie Morrow had agreed to see him, despite his assurances to Liz that he'd be unable to resist.

Charlie had kept him guessing until late on the Sunday night, then called to say he could fit him in on the Monday morning.

'Fit him in.' Macey had laughed at that. As if the man had anything better to do.

Macey had some trouble offloading his scheduled work, but he managed it and arrived at the nursing home, Liz in tow, just after eleven.

Charlie was waiting for them in the lounge, positioned so that he could watch them arrive through the half-open door. He watched Macey's reaction as the nurse pointed the way through and the journalist caught sight of him, the livid scars puckering the right side of his face and the pressure bandages on his hands and upper body just visible beneath his shirt.

He gave Macey eight out of ten for control, the way he put aside his shock and strode forward, businesslike and brisk, with his hand extended. The girl following behind was less able to hide her reaction, but Charlie didn't object to the frank way she looked at him. Anyway, she had pretty eyes and a body that invited equal notice, so he considered it a reasonable trade.

Macey sat down opposite Charlie and glanced around. 'Posh place,' he said. 'Private, is it?'

Morrow laughed. 'My wife took out health insurance years ago. We've been divorced for more than a decade so that'll tell you how long. The payments went out direct debit and somehow I never got around to cancelling. I thought it was time they gave me something back.'

'Not public money, then? Police charity fund or something?'

'No, so feel free to splash it across the headlines. Hero cop goes private.'

Macey made a show of writing it down, then grinned at Liz. 'Grab that table and bring it over here,' he said to her. 'That's unless you'd like to go somewhere else, Charlie?'

'No one's going to bother us,' Charlie assured him. 'I'm an acerbic bugger and they leave me alone. Now, what have you got for me?'

It had been a condition of Macey's visit that he bring Charlie up to date on the Bowen case and Liz had spent a good two hours with the photocopier, making a record of Macey's archive. She'd piled it into a black pilot's case, which she now proceeded to empty onto the coffee table. Charlie eased forward in his chair, eyes gleaming with anticipation.

'Your copies of everything I have,' Macey told him. 'Enjoy. Now, do you mind if I tape this, or should we make Liz do her bit with the shorthand?'

*

Jane Adams

The incident with Peterson's family had disturbed Mike deeply. He left them comforting each other and discussing the safest course of action while he tried to get through to Maria on his mobile phone. She was with a patient, he was told, and couldn't be disturbed. He thought about insisting, but it seemed a little pointless. What could he tell her beyond the fact that she should take extra care?

And that she should check on Essie.

He had Maria's mother's number somewhere, he remembered, but it was back at his office and, anyway, the same thing applied. What could he tell them? In the end he called John Tynan and filled him in briefly on what had happened, reluctant to say too much over the air.

'I'll keep trying Maria,' John promised. 'In fact, I'll go over there. She's off duty today at four or thereabouts.'

Mike thanked him. 'I'm probably just being paranoid,' he said.

'No, you're just being human,' John told him. 'And it's human to worry about those we love.'

'They wouldn't let me see anything or tell me anything in the hospital,' Charlie was complaining. 'I understand why, but it didn't make it any easier. Wouldn't even let me watch the bloody news. Afraid it might upset me. *Upset me!* I'm still a bloody copper, aren't I? He didn't stop my mind working even if he did have a go at blowing my bloody face off.'

Macey grinned at him, sensing a kindred spirit. 'Charlie, my friend,' he said, 'we have to work together.'

Charlie snorted. 'Me? Work with a flaming journalist? Lowest of the frigging low?' Then he smiled, half his mouth pulled crooked by the scars. 'What do you have in mind?'

By the time Macey and Liz left, Macey had promised to provide Charlie with computer equipment and a modem. He had his own phone line in his room – 'one of the perks of going private, though they'll probably crib about the phone bill' – so there would be no problem setting up the Internet access that Charlie would need.

Charlie Morrow might not be able to get out there looking for Jake Bowen on the streets, but Macey had given him another option. Macey had been scanning the news groups on the Net, looking for mention of Bowen and his exploits. There was plenty out there. The police already had people trawling the Internet, but Charlie felt he had a slight edge, something that might lead Bowen to make contact. He'd let Macey write his report, take photographs, give vent to much of Charlie's resentment and pain, and both Charlie and Macey would have put money on Jake Bowen reading every word and responding. Anything, they felt at this stage, would be worth a try. It would give Charlie an in on the action and Macey would write the exclusive. Setting up an e-mail address could be done quickly and it would give Jake Bowen yet another point of contact. Charlie hoped against hope that he would strike lucky and Jake Bowen would take the bait.

'Can you manage a keyboard?' Liz asked anxiously, looking at Charlie's hands.

'Don't worry, love,' he told her, his eyes alive with excitement now he was taking part. 'I'll manage, and I can still point and click a flaming mouse.'

It had taken Mike a couple of hours to get to Exeter, dropping off the photographs on the way and collecting a WPC to take with him to the Normans.

Julia's parents lived in a quiet suburban road of 1930s houses: twinned, bay-fronted semis with neat gardens. Already an hour late for his original appointment, he had called them on the way to apologize. But as he had become lost in the tangle of side-streets that bore no resemblance to the A–Z, that time had almost doubled.

Frank Norman met him at the door but paid little attention to his apology.

'We'd nowhere else to go, Inspector,' he said quietly. 'I'll show you her room.'

No one spoke as the grey-haired man led them up the stairs and along the short landing. Julia's room was at the back of the house, overlooking the garden. He opened the door and then turned back along the corridor.

'If you've anything to ask, we'll be downstairs,' he said. He didn't even glance into his daughter's room.

Mike and the WPC, Annie Poyser, stood just inside the door and looked around. He had intended for her to speak with the Normans while he checked Julia's room, but that no longer seemed appropriate. Frank Norman was intent on calling the shots.

'It's pretty,' Annie commented. 'My mum and dad have a place like this but I was always stuck in the box room and you couldn't swing a cat.'

Mike smiled at her. 'The advantages of being an only child.'

'Tidier than my place too, but I don't suppose she was here that much.'

'They said weekends, sometimes. And Sunday lunch, apparently. They didn't like her missing that.'

Annie laughed. 'Sunday lunch with a hangover,' she said. 'O joy.' She frowned, moving across to the window and glancing out over the lawned garden. A child's swing still took pride of place down at the far end. 'Didn't like her growing up,' she commented. 'And the room, too, it's kind of childish, all pink and white like this.'

Mike looked around with a fresh eye. Annie was right. The decor of the room, with its cake-icing colours and frilled flowery curtains, was almost babyish. It was unsophisticated and shamelessly pretty, only the blue of the bedcover jarring oddly with the rest of the scheme.

'There's nothing personal here,' he commented. 'I mean, even if she only stayed over at the weekends, you'd have expected, I don't know, pictures, ornaments . . . something.'

Annie was opening the dressing-table drawers. A few items of underwear, a comb and a lipstick in one. Nothing in the other. The small chest of drawers was similarly empty, just two T-shirts, a hairbrush, a few cosmetics. The built-in wardrobe still had its hangers and a winter coat. There was an overnight bag on the floor.

Mike picked it up, set it on the bed and began to sort through the pockets. Annie was taking the lining papers from the drawers, turning the drawers themselves upside down in case something had been taped to the underside, running a hand around the empty spaces left in the dressing table.

Mike gave up on the bag. 'Anything?'

''Fraid not, sir.'

They checked the back of the dressing table and the mirrors, lifted the furniture to look beneath and stripped the covers from the bed and the mattress from the frame.

'Not even the fluff monster,' Annie commented. 'I mean, it's as if the whole place's been thoroughly cleaned. There's not a speck of dust even.'

Mike looked at her and realized that she was right. He led the way back down the stairs. The Normans were in the kitchen, sitting motionless on either side of the table, looking like awkward strangers in what had once been their home.

'Did you find anything, Inspector?' Frank Norman asked.

'That isn't likely, is it, Mr Norman?'

Frank looked across at his wife and reached for her hand. 'I'm sorry,' he said. 'I should have said something. I should have stopped her, but I was only gone a little while, just to the corner shop to get some milk and she'd . . .'

Tears filled his eyes and he pointed out towards the garden. 'Near the swing,' he said. 'There's a steel basket there I use for burning garden stuff.'

Mike gestured for Annie to go and look, then he drew another chair close to the table. 'Why did you burn her things, Mrs Norman? What was it?'

'She even took the bedclothes off the bed,' Frank told him. 'Burned the lot. It was the pictures. Julia like some cheap . . .' He shook his head. 'Not our Julie,' he whispered. 'Not our girl. Then, well, I knew you wanted to see her room. I knew you'd be coming and I thought—' he looked at Mike. 'I thought, it's not my Julie they're after. If I made it look like it was supposed to, odd bits she might have left behind, then you wouldn't pry. There's enough been done to her already, Inspector, we just wanted the rest left alone now.'

'It's still destruction of evidence, Mr Norman. It was still something that might have helped us find your daughter's killer.' He broke off. Anger was pointless now.

He walked down the garden to where Annie was sifting through the ashes, trying not to add to the ruin that had already taken place. It was starting to rain, fat droplets of water splashing onto the back of Mike's neck.

'Photos mostly,' Annie told him, 'but there's quite a bit not burned right through.' She glanced up at the darkening clouds. 'We ought to get this covered up, sir. A rainstorm'll just about finish what's left.'

'There are bags in the boot of the car,' Mike said. He waited in the now heavy rain for Annie to come running back and help him pile the remains of Mrs Norman's bonfire into the black bags, their gloved hands soon slippery with wet soot and their clothes covered with ash, but even in their haste Mike could glimpse the images that had given Julia's mother so much pain.

Essie's grandmother, May Richards, went to collect her from school. It was a small building, red-brick, slate-roofed, built in the 1920s. Mobile classrooms had been added as the population had grown and these stood to one side of the main building near the Abbot Street gate. Essie's class was in one of them and May could see Essie through the window as she passed by, busy painting at an easel, daubing bright colours onto a large sheet of paper with the frowning concentration of a true artist.

May laughed and risked a wave, but Essie didn't see. She then crossed the playground to the other gate at the Long Street end. The school had outgrown its original capacity and home time was always chaos. To minimize the problem, the smaller children came out of the Long Street gate, where the road was quieter and there was more space for those with pushchairs and smaller siblings to stand.

May was well known. She'd lived all her life in the area, gone to this school and often came with her daughter Jo to collect Essie. She stood chatting with the waiting parents, glancing across the playground now and then, waiting for her grandchild to appear.

Essie was never among the first out. She was a popular child and always slow at getting her coat on and her shoes fastened, because she was too busy playing, so it was only when the crowds of children had thinned and

May had already seen several of Essie's friends go by that she began to worry.

Concerned that if she left the gate, Essie might miss her, she hung on, staring intently at each child that passed, asking ones she knew if they had seen Essie, until finally the playground emptied and May hurried across to the mobile.

The teacher looked up in surprise as May burst through the door. 'Mrs Richards? Is something wrong?'

They searched everywhere – the toilets, the grounds, the main school. Staff went out into the street to call after the late leavers straggling their way home.

Then they called the police. There was no doubt of it: Essie had gone.

A message had been left on Mike's voice-mail about an hour before. Mike had been with the Normans, talking about another missing child, and his messages had been ignored.

This one said, 'She's a pretty little thing, Mike. Very photogenic, don't you think?'

Chapter Nine

It was late evening by the time Mike reached Norwich and drove straight to May Richards's house.

He had managed to speak to Maria about an hour after Essie had first disappeared. At that point no one at the Norwich end knew about Jake's message and the hope was still that she might just have wandered away. As out of character as that was, it was the most comforting thought, though from the outset Maria had insisted she tell the investigating officers about Mike and the possible involvement of Jake Bowen. The anxiety and fear were palpable as Mike spoke to the young officer at the front door.

Maria heard his voice and came through into the hall.

'I don't think you should be here,' she said. 'Wait for me at John's and I'll talk to you later.'

'I've driven here to be with you,' he objected.

'And I have to be with my family, Mike, and I'm afraid you're not someone they want to see right now.'

'They blame me,' Mike said flatly.

'I'm sorry. It's not your fault.' But he could hear the doubt in her voice. 'Look, I blame myself. If I hadn't brought Essie with me at the weekend, she might still be here.'

'You think Jake Bowen doesn't know about you?

About your family? Do you think it would have made any difference? Maria, he's got the inside track on everyone who's come even close to him.'

'Then no one's safe, anywhere,' Maria said.

She then turned away from him and went back down the hall, leaving him utterly bereft.

'She's just really upset, sir,' the officer by the door said to him, trying to offer comfort. 'Her sister, the little girl's mum, she's discharged herself from hospital. She just can't stop crying.'

Mike nodded and slipped quietly out through the front door. He'd expected blame. Anticipated the raw anger that the situation was bound to generate, but had never thought he would be excluded like this. It was worse than anything he had prepared himself for.

Getting into his car, he thought of Stevie, his son; of the drunk driver who'd taken his child from him and never even stopped to help. It was something he could not recover from and he knew that a little part of him had died along with his son.

But this. For someone to deliberately take a child, to deprive the parents and to let them suffer, not knowing if their baby was already dead or still alive and frightened or in pain.

He thought of Julia Norman and his hands shook as he turned the key in the ignition, barely able to cope any more with the thoughts running through his head.

Mike phoned Peterson from John Tynan's. His daughter and grandchildren had left, he said, gone north to stay with relatives. He wasn't certain it would help, but that was the best they could do. 'I've been promised police protection for them, but it's hard to know what to do for the best. Any news your end?'

'Nothing. There's nothing yet. I feel like I'm in limbo here. I can't get involved in the investigation and I can't help Essie's family. They don't want me around.'

'Then come back here, where you can at least be some use. I'm sorry, Mike, but even if you applied for compassionate leave I'd have to veto it. I can't spare you.'

Mike sighed, guiltily relieved to have had the decision of what to do next taken out of his hands.

'Essie's just a child,' he said. 'She's five years old.'

'And we've no record of Bowen ever attacking children. We have to hope this is just some kind of stunt to get our attention.'

'What about the photographs your daughter received?'

'Photo images, expertly tampered with. Damn it, Mike, we even know what software he probably used. It doesn't mean . . .'

'But the threat is there. Inherent.'

'Yes,' Peterson allowed, the threat was there. 'But for Christ's sake, Mike, if we let ourselves think along those lines . . . We've got to function. If I thought that little girl . . . If I thought about my grandchildren . . .' He broke off.

Mike could think of nothing more to say. Gently, silently, he put the receiver down.

Chapter Ten

It was early on Tuesday morning when Mike called Maria and told her that he would be going back to Honiton.

'If you want me to stay, then I'll stay,' he told her. 'If you want me to, then I will.'

'Go back, Mike. There's nothing you can do here and it's important you keep working on this. It's the best thing you can do for Essie.'

Mike's heart sank. Even though she was right and he remembered Peterson's words of the night before, he had still hoped that she would want him with her.

'There's no more news?' he asked.

'Nothing. That's what's so hard to take. We're just waiting. The doctor's given Jo a sedative and she's sleeping a lot, then she wakes up feeling guilty about going to sleep. And Moma and I, we can't do anything. It's so hard, Mike, we sit around doing nothing and feeling like death, but if one of us puts the TV on or tries to read, we feel as though we're being frivolous or thoughtless, when what we should be doing is giving 100 per cent of our thoughts to Essie and Jo. I thought I'd cope better than this. I spend my entire life teaching other people to cope.'

'But this time it's you and yours,' Mike put in gently. 'It's not the same.' He paused, then asked, 'Can I at least see you before I go?'

She hesitated for a moment, then said reluctantly, 'I can't leave just now and you can't come here. It would be more than Jo could bear. You must realize that.'

Mike arrived back at the incident room in Honiton after a long, hot drive. He drove badly, far too fast on narrow, winding roads, the miles passing with little conscious thought or recognition on his part.

He reached Honiton mid-afternoon, tired and angry. His shirt was sticking to his back and he was suddenly aware that it had been at least two days since he had last shaved.

Peterson wanted to see him, he was told, as soon as he came in. Mike found him in one of the interview rooms, sitting at the table with a man Mike did not recognize. They were leafing through the copies of Harriman's cuttings books, the stranger poring over them intently while Peterson sat back in his chair as though to distance himself from the other man. He had an air about him of scarcely concealed anger and looked up sharply as Mike entered the room.

'Mike. Good. I want to introduce you to someone.' The other man stood up and turned towards Mike, his hand already extended. As he made the introductions, Peterson's anger began to bubble over, giving a harsh edge to his words.

'This,' he said, 'is Mr Alastair Bowen. Father to the famous Jake. Perhaps you'd like to explain to Inspector Croft just why it took you so long to come forward, Mr Bowen.'

Alastair Bowen's expression was one of total calm. 'As I told you, Mr Peterson,' he said, 'it was because of my wife. My wife, you see, was dying. I had to stay with her and I could not bear that she should know about Jake. Not after all he'd put her through before.' He sighed. 'But she's dead now, after two long years of suffering, God rest her soul, and I can speak. Tell you about my son.'

'We're glad to hear that, Mr Bowen,' Peterson said, 'as, I'm sure, will be the parents and families of those your son has killed these last months, while you were waiting for the right moment.'

Alastair Bowen continued to regard Peterson with the same calm gaze, his grey eyes gentle and unmoved by the outburst.

'I don't expect you to understand,' he said, 'and I have no intention of making excuses that no one wants to hear. But I am here now, Superintendent, and that, believe me, is all that really counts.'

Chapter Eleven

Mike flicked through the photographs in the folder and laid one down in front of Alastair Bowen. It was five o'clock and the late afternoon sun streaming in through the window mocked the grossness of the images.

'Marion O'Donnel,' he said.

Obediently Alastair regarded the image of the pretty blonde woman set before him.

'And this is how she ended up, Mr Bowen.' He covered the picture with another showing a burnt-out car and the remains of a body curled grotesquely in the driver's seat.

'She was one of his so-called models, I suppose.'

'She was,' Mike told him.

Alastair shrugged.

'You're suggesting she deserved to die like this, Mr Bowen?'

'You lie down with wolves, Inspector.'

Mike let it pass, but his dislike of Alastair Bowen was growing by the second. Two hours they had spent so far, bringing Alastair up to date on Jake's crimes, trying to draw from the man some kind of response, some kind of explanation for what his son was doing. They were looking for a clue that might help them to predict his next move.

'This one's from February.' Peterson laid the photograph of another young woman down on the table. She too was blonde, her long hair wrapped tightly around her throat, hiding the bruises left by her killer's hands. 'We don't even know her name,' he said. 'But somewhere she has family, friends who want to know what happened to her.'

'You believe that?' Alastair questioned. 'In their place I'd prefer to keep my illusions, not be faced with the life she must have led.'

'Whatever life she led, Mr Bowen, she was still a young woman who had the right to live it.'

'I didn't kill her, Superintendent Peterson,' Alastair retorted impassively. 'I don't need your accusations.'

'This next is Simon Caldwell,' Mike went on. 'He was twenty-eight years old. An actor.'

'Is that what you call it? Acting?'

'An actor, Mr Bowen. Jake killed him by forcing a tube down into his stomach and feeding him neat bleach. It's a horrific way to die, Alastair.'

'My wife died of cancer, Inspector. That is a horrific way to die. Death is rarely either clean or peaceful.'

'This is hardly the same as death caused by illness, Mr Bowen.'

'And you expect me to have more sympathy with this actor than with the sick who die of disease not of their making? He chose the way he lived.'

'He didn't choose the way he died.'

'How many of us do? How many of us could?'

Mike gave up and pushed the photograph aside. Caldwell's professional name had been a little more ana-tomically biased. He'd been starring in porn flicks the past five years, making a steady living out of his knack for staying hard as long as the producer wanted. Caldwell had kept his reputation right up until the time he died, and the ligature tied around his penis made certain that he stayed that way.

'Matthew Thompson,' Mike went on impassively, laying the next image on the table. 'Not one of Jake's actors, as far as we know. He was a businessman, owned a chain of retail outlets.'

Alastair Bowen glanced at the picture. 'I remember the news item,' he said. 'The man died in his bath, I believe.'

Mike nodded. 'He'd been tied up. Tied up with a wire noose round his neck. The end had been fastened to the drain hole and the hole blocked with car body-filler. Jake must have been in his flat for quite some time to set this one up. The man had been drugged, presumably while Jake stripped him and positioned him in the bath. Then he'd turned on the taps and left them running. We know Jake watched him die because we have the film.' It was not something Mike would forget in any hurry. 'He watched him die and he filmed every moment, Alastair.' The man struggling to get free before the water drowned him or the ligature tightened around his neck and he choked to death.

Mike thought of Essie, then tried not to think of Essie. He turned angrily on Alastair Bowen.

'There's no pattern to what he does. His victims are all different. Male, female, all ages, no real consistent MO. And we need to get him, Alastair, before he kills again. Before he kills ... that child.' Mike found he choked on Essie's name.

'And you expect me to explain it to you? You expect me to explain my son?'

'Any light you should shed. We need anything you can give us,' Peterson told him.

Alastair Bowen made no response. He stared at the pictures on the table but seemed not to see them.

'Jake sees himself as an artist,' he said at last. 'He'd do whatever was needed to get an effect. It was always that way.' He looked up at Mike. 'He's also a business-man, Inspector Croft. Surely you lot have worked that out by now? Jake works to commission, he always did. Someone wants a particular script filming and is willing to pay top price for it, Jake will do it any way they want. Life doesn't matter to him. People's lives, their hopes, it's all script to Jake. All part of the storyline.'

'You know this for certain?'

Alastair Bowen pushed himself away from the table, irritated and clearly bored. 'A child could work it out, Inspector Croft. You've detailed Jake's career, you've seen the films. Jake enjoys what he does, but he also makes a killing from it, if you'll excuse the pun, and you can bet your sweet life that he's been doing it for a hell of a lot longer than you credit him with.'

There had been the problem of finding somewhere for Alastair Bowen to stay, but finally they had settled him at Lyme in the boarding house that Maria had stayed in with Essie. There was a room available only for the next two nights, but there was talk anyway of moving Alastair to a safe house as soon as they went public with him. It seemed logical to assume that Jake would not appreciate his father giving evidence against him.

Mike then made his way slowly back towards the Dorchester road.

It was almost ten p.m. and the sky already darkening over a calm sea. Bats cruised in front of him as he travelled the back roads heading towards the dual carriageway. There was little other traffic and nothing in the blue-grey of the twilight to distract him. Mike was very tired. His thoughts began to wander. Twice he caught himself nodding with sleep, jerking his attention back only just in time as he veered across the road.

He tried to drag his thoughts to the case. Thinking about the fragmentary photographs that they had found at the Normans' house. He doubted they would help further the investigation. All they had done so far was cause more pain to the parents. The few items she had left at the house she shared when she went away had added little to their knowledge. There had been sketches, notebooks for her college projects. No portraits and nothing relating to Jake, not even the odd initialled heart scribbled in the margins. Jake must have been one big secret in Julia Norman's life.

'She was seeing someone,' one of the girls she had lived with had said. 'We knew that, and we thought it must be someone older. But, I mean, Julia went out with a lot of boys, none of them got serious.'

The impression was that Julia had been sowing a few wild oats, breaking free of her parents' rather staid and solid background. When he had put this to her flatmates, one of the girls had laughed. 'Oh, God. Yeah, I guess that's what Julia thought she was doing, but I mean, really, if she had more than a couple of drinks she'd see it as living on the edge.' She'd hesitated, close to tears. 'She was sweet, you know. Innocent.'

The fork for the main road came up out of nowhere and took Mike by surprise. He swerved onto it, blessing the fact that the road was deserted at this time of night. Driving between the trees, it was darker and his mind began to wander yet again. From the corner of his eye he caught movement between the trees like someone running, leaping from the shadow of one tree to the next. He wound the window down and put the radio on, finding some local station playing loud rock music, then flicked the lights to full beam to drive the shadow-men away. For a minute or two it seemed to work, but then he nodded again, his eyes began to close and even the music faded, the names and faces of the dead filling his mind as he drifted into sleep. Julia, Marion O'Donnel, Caldwell, Matthew Thompson. Essie . . . No, his mind rebelled against that one. No, not Essie!

It was the jolt of the front wheel hitting the verge that woke him and the sudden jerk of the seat-belt cutting across his chest. For one God-awful moment Mike thought . . .

Wearily, he stumbled from the car and stood in the road waiting for his breath to slow down and his heart to stop pounding. The car was poised with one wheel above the ditch and the first of the trees only inches away.

Chapter Twelve

True to his word Macey had taken the computer equipment to Charlie Morrow. He'd arrived early and the morning news was on in Charlie's room. The two men watched in silence as the hastily arranged press conference was aired and pictures of five-year-old Essie filled the screen.

'There has been no word from the kidnapper and, so far, no clue as to why this child was taken. Essie's grandmother and aunt made the following appeal to the kidnapper . . .'

Macey and Charlie continued to watch, listening as the two women made tearful appeals that the child be given back, that she not be hurt, that she be left somewhere for the police to find. They had heard it all before. Neither spoke until the news moved on.

'Poor little bugger,' Macey said softly. 'Not much hope there, I don't suppose.' He frowned. 'But I've seen that woman before. The aunt, I mean, I just can't quite place her.'

'She's Mike Croft's girlfriend,' Charlie told him, his voice harsh with shock.

'Then Jake must have taken the child,' Macey said.

Mike had watched the appeal on the early news. Afterwards, he had tried again to call Maria, only to find that she had left to go to Oaklands and collect some things. He guessed she also needed time away from the overwhelming tension of it all. He tried Oaklands, where Maria lived and worked, to find that he'd just missed her. Her mobile was switched off, which meant she was probably in her car, and he was forced to give up.

He called her mother's house again and left a message with the officer on duty, asking him to get her to phone.

'She tried earlier,' he was told, 'but you were in a meeting and she couldn't reach you.'

Mike smiled faintly. At least she'd tried. 'Tell her to use my mobile number. And to keep trying. I'll leave the damned thing switched on.'

He rang off, deeply frustrated. This seemed to be the pattern of their relationship just now, missing one another . . .

It had taken a long time to persuade Alastair Bowen that he should go public, but he had finally agreed and much of Mike's day had been taken up with the arrangements.

'People will hate me,' Alastair had said. 'They will hate me for what I am. They will blame me for Jake.'

'They'll hate you more if you don't,' Peterson told him bluntly. 'Alastair, you're the best hope we've got, the first real advantage we've had on Jake. You appearing on the television may be just what we need to flush him out.'

Finally, he had given in and after that everything had

moved with speed. The *Ten o'clock News* saw Alastair Bowen on national television, patched in from BBC Bristol and simultaneously broadcast as a newsflash on all channels. Alastair Bowen pleading with his son to put an end to the killing and the pain.

'I'm asking you to come forward, Jake. There's been enough death and enough cruelty. You need help, Jake, as much as anyone else, you need help and I promise I'll be there for you, whatever you might have done.'

He hesitated, clearly uncertain of how to carry on. 'Your mother's dead. She died five days ago from cancer and I buried her back home at St Bartolph's. I know she missed you . . . son . . . we both did, and thought about you . . . always. It's time to come home.'

Watching from the sidelines, Mike could see the falsity of Alastair Bowen's pleas.

He despises him, he thought. Loathes and fears Jake even more than we do. It was a revelation, a small one, but, Mike felt, deeply significant. He set himself the task of finding out why and when Alastair had first conceived this passionate loathing of his son.

Jake Bowen had not expected ever to see his father alive and his appearance on the late news caught him by surprise.

Sitting on the large blue sofa in front of the television, Jake leaned forward to get a closer look at the parent he had left behind so many years before.

He swivelled round to regard the small figure lying propped on pillows at the other end of the settee.

'Don't you think he's getting old?' Jake asked the child.

Essie, arms limply at her sides and eyes gazing listlessly into space, never said a word.

Chapter Thirteen

Early on the Wednesday morning Mike took Alastair Bowen to see Max Harriman.

Alastair was confident. 'He'll speak to me,' he assured Mike, with that same implacable calm he had displayed when Mike had first been introduced. 'Max loved Jake, doted on him. I'm a link back to their shared past, you see. Max will speak with me.'

Mike was not so sure. Harriman had a mind of his own where cooperation was concerned.

Alastair seemed less blasé about the news reports that had followed his appearance on the television the night before. Every national led with some version of the story, the headlines varying from the lurid 'Father of a Monster' to the insipid 'News Appeal Brings Fresh Hope'. All asked why Alastair Bowen had taken so long to come forward. All seemed certain that he must long ago have known what path his son had taken.

Mike asked him about it as they drove along the M5, keeping just above the speed limit in the centre lane.

'I knew he was involved with filth,' Alastair told him. 'That he made films that decent people would never want to see.'

'Was that what made you break with him?' Mike asked. 'We know he lived with you into his early twenties, then you and your wife and Jake seem to drop out of sight. What happened then, Mr Bowen?'

Alastair took time before he answered. His reply, when it came, was obtuse. 'Jake was evil. From the moment he was born, the boy was evil. I told his mother, but she wouldn't have it. No, she was a good woman and could see good in everyone, even Jake. But it was there, that devil's look, right from the moment he was born and I first looked into his eyes.'

Mike glanced sideways at him, the hairs rising at the back of his neck, despite the absurdity of Alastair Bowen's words.

'I don't believe that any child is born evil,' he replied. 'Children are a blank page, it's what the world does to them that makes them good or bad.'

'A *tabula rasa*,' Alastair intoned. He laughed. 'Inspector Croft, I would have thought you'd seen enough of the world to know the lie of that. Sometimes evil is born, made incarnate, and there is nothing you can do to that child, neither kindness nor beating, that can make it not so.'

Mike shifted uncomfortably in his seat. 'And what did Jake have most of, Mr Bowen? Kindness or beating?'

Again the laughter devoid of humour. 'Oh, no, Inspector, you can't lay that at my door. No one can say that Jake was made the way he is by anything I did to him. Jake had what was needed, one way or another, in about equal measure. His mother was too soft with him. Women are. I had to balance that. But he respected me for it even though I knew there would be no saving him. I had to try, you see, for his mother's sake. What woman would want to live with the fact that she'd given birth to evil?'

Mike glanced at the dashboard clock and saw that there would be at least another hour before they reached Max Harriman. He wondered how much more of Bowen's ranting he could take, but there was so much he needed to know. He tried another tack.

'Max's mother. She brought him up alone, I understand?'

He felt rather than saw Alastair Bowen nod. 'The father was killed in a mining accident just before the boy was born. It put her into labour early and they weren't sure she or the boy would have the will to live.'

He fell silent.

Mike persisted. 'Mrs Harriman was killed about the time that you and Jake left the area?'

'That is true.'

'And Max was accused, taken in for questioning.'

'And then released without charge.'

'Did Jake kill Mrs Harriman?' Mike asked.

Alastair was silent, so silent and so still that Mike thought he might even have fallen asleep. He glanced sideways at him once more. The man sat with his hands clasped neatly in his lap and an empty expression on his face, gazing out through the windscreen at the road ahead.

'Mr Bowen?' Mike prompted. 'Do you think Jake killed her?'

Alastair shifted slightly in his seat, but took his time making a reply. 'I never saw that woman smile,' he said.

*

Macey paid another visit to Charlie Morrow, this time bringing him a pile of disks; stuff he'd pulled down from the Net.

'Mostly news groups and chat rooms,' he said. 'We know Jake Bowen puts stuff out over the Internet. If he's online then he must have a provider and most providers monitor anyone making an abnormal number of hits to kinky sites.'

'Most, but not all,' Charlie corrected him, 'and there are ways around it. Depends on the route you take through the system. Anyone as smart as Jake Bowen will have thought of that. So, for that matter, will my untoasted colleagues.'

'Right,' Macey said. He'd still not grown used to the way Charlie made fun of his injuries. 'Look, he went on, I've been trying something a bit different. As you know, there are chat rooms and discussion groups on just about anything. I've picked up over a dozen without even trying hard, all specializing in kinky porn, and they've all got something to say about Jake Bowen.'

'With or without prompting?' Charlie asked.

'Bit of both. My whole point is, you can sit on the side, monitor a few. Folk out there still have the illusion that they can say just about anything online, like they forget it's a public place. See what you can stir up.'

He delved into his briefcase and pulled out a computer magazine with a CD still attached to the front.

'*America On-line*,' he said triumphantly. 'One month's free connection, complete with helpline. All you've got to do is pay for the calls. Here, keep the mag. Present from me to you.'

Charlie gave him that crooked half-smile that looked more like anger. 'You're all heart, Macey,' he said.

Max Harriman was not pleased. He had recognized Alastair Bowen almost immediately, despite the years, and his reaction thereafter had ranged from the sulky to the outraged.

'Why bring *him* here?' he wanted to know. 'He doesn't know a thing about Jake. He abandoned him years ago. Some father he was.'

'He's told me more about Jake than you have,' Mike lied. 'Maybe you'd like to set the record straight, Max. Maybe I should tell you what Alastair here's been saying and you can put us right?'

Max sank into an angry silence and refused to be drawn. Mike stood up.

'Well, if you won't talk to me then I think I'll go now. After all, it doesn't look as if we'll be needing you so much now, does it?'

Max was on his feet and yelling loud enough to bring the guards. 'He knows nothing!' he shouted. 'I'm the one that Jake came to. I'm the one that studied him, that followed after him – that understands him. They never did. Never. You need *me*, Inspector Mike Croft, and don't you forget it.'

Mike wondered briefly whether to push his advantage or to let Max simmer. The ringing of his mobile decided for him and he allowed the guards to take an irate Max and escort him back to his cell.

The call was from Peterson, who'd heard from Julia Norman's parents. A video film of her had arrived in the morning post.

The journey back with Alastair Bowen was a very quiet one, both men busy with their own thoughts. It was only when Mike dropped him at the safe house they had put him into after the TV broadcast that Alastair referred to their earlier talk.

'I always thought he'd done it,' he said. 'Killed Emily Harriman. Jake was always round there and the woman liked him.' He paused. 'Women did like him,' he said, 'all women.'

'Why did you suspect him?'

The man hesitated. 'Because of the blood,' he said. 'Jake came home with blood on his hands and the cuffs of his sleeves. The papers said she'd had her throat cut and everyone knows that would send blood everywhere, so I thought I must have been mistaken.'

'And his jacket?' Mike asked. 'Was he wearing a jacket? Mrs Harriman was attacked from behind, her throat cut, and then she was dropped to the floor, her assailant still behind her. Yes, there would have been a lot of blood, but not necessarily all over Jake. Mostly his hands, his cuffs, the sleeves of his jacket.'

'He said he lost his jacket,' Alastair Bowen

remarked, staring out of the car window as if absorbed by the scene.

'And you said nothing?' Mike asked him.

'And I said nothing,' Alastair Bowen agreed.

Peterson was waiting for him in the barn-cum-incident room at Colwell Barton.

'Have fun with Max and Alastair?' he asked.

'Oh, yes, great company. Two of a kind.'

'Maybe they should form a double act when Max gets out. But seriously, did you learn anything?'

'Beyond Alastair Bowen being a religious nut?' He sat down heavily, watching as Peterson set the video player. 'Yes, I learned that Max is jealous and that gives us leverage. And that Jake probably started his career early.'

'With Mrs Harriman, as we thought?'

Mike nodded thoughtfully, but there was clearly something else on his mind.

'I don't like what you're thinking, Mike.'

He smiled at the familiar phraseology. 'It's the way Alastair talked about it. He said that Jake came home with his hands and cuffs covered with blood and his jacket missing. I mean, agreed Jake lived only a couple of streets away from the Harrimans and agreed it was late and dark and probably there was no one to see him on the way home, but why not take time to wash his hands? He must have known it was possible his parents were at home. It was as if he wanted his father to see. A challenge, if you like.'

'If that's so, and I think you may be on to something, why lose the jacket?'

Mike shrugged. 'I don't know,' he said. 'Why do any of the things Jake does? It's as if he was constantly trying to keep everyone off balance even then.'

'It could be you're looking too deep,' Peterson suggested. 'Maybe he just panicked and ran, threw the jacket away and didn't realize how much blood there was until he got home.'

'Maybe. But no, I don't think so. The jacket was never found and the area was searched thoroughly. And you've got to remember, this isn't an affluent area. People might have a work jacket, an everyday one and one for Sundays if they were lucky. I remember my dad had the same Sunday clothes for years.'

Peterson laughed. 'Sounds like me,' he said. 'But I hear what you're saying. Clothes weren't just thrown away and the locals would recognize something that was. It would have led them straight to Jake.'

He sat down beside Mike, playing with the video remote.

'You think he killed before that,' Peterson said thoughtfully, 'and that his father knew about it. That leaving the blood on his hands for his father to see was like saying, "Look at me, there's nothing you can do", something like that?'

Mike nodded. 'Yes. And I think it's important we find out who and when. It might give us the opening we're looking for.'

'It might, and it might just waste a lot more time. Oh, I think you're right, Mike, but we've got enough on our plates dealing with the current Jake Bowen, never mind raking through his distant past.'

He set the video to play.

Jake Bowen still had to work, no matter what else he was involved in. His film-making and other activities he saw as a profitable sideline – very profitable and invested wisely. Jake had learned early, though, that you should always have a good cover story, that people quickly become suspicious of someone with no regular lifestyle or habits or obvious source of income, and Jake had always had a 'proper job' and made certain that, superficially at any rate, he lived within his means.

Jake was content to wait. He was saving hard for his retirement, and planned on making it a long and easy one.

His proper job just now was as a sales rep for an artists' supply house. He enjoyed it. It involved meeting people and selling, two things Jake was very good at. And it gave him opportunity for a little talent-spotting on the side.

Jake knew his stuff. He was way ahead of the game with the latest colours, always knowing which pigment or primer or paper would give the best results; always helpful and willing to go that extra mile to get a satisfied customer. And he was knowledgeable enough to suggest alternatives for hard-to-get supplies or willing to push his buyers into obtaining things for him.

As Mike and Peterson were viewing the video of Julia

Norman, Jake was leaving the Fine Arts Department at Exeter University. The young woman who'd been tutor to Julia Norman waved to him from her window as he left, the new samples and colour charts he'd just brought in piled on her desk.

Such a very nice man, she thought idly, turning the ring on her engagement finger and wondering if he was single.

Chapter Fourteen

There was something like forty-five minutes of film, much of it gently erotic and strangely compelling. The first ten minutes or so were images that could have been on anyone's home movie.

They were shot on a near-deserted beach: a windy day and Julia, her long hair flying loose as she ran towards the camera. She wore jeans and a shapeless blue sweater, the wind strong enough to mould it to her body as she performed, pretending she didn't want to be filmed, but dancing barefoot on the sands, teasing the film-maker.

Much of their shouted dialogue was lost, whipped away on the strong wind, but Julia chatted to Jake, laughed with him, completely at ease and, Mike thought as he looked into her eyes, clearly in love with him.

They couldn't hear the joke that Julia told, but they heard Jake laugh, the microphone built into the camera easily picking up the sound. Mike was shocked at the naturalness of it, the ease and happiness he heard, as though Jake had not a care in the world, and no plans for anything but enjoyment with this girl.

Other scenes followed, some in which Julia participated with full knowledge, some in which she was clearly unaware that she was being filmed. It was as though Jake wanted to catch her every unconscious movement, her naturalness when she thought herself unobserved. Julia in the park, throwing bread to the ducks. Julia sitting on the steps outside her shared house, chatting to one of her room-mates. Julia brushing her hair and putting on lipstick. Julia painting the canvas she had given her parents that last Christmas.

Peterson paused the film at that point and tried to take it through frame by frame, cursing the scanning lines that ran across the image and his inability to hold the picture steady on the cheap VCR they'd brought with them to the barn. It was good enough, though, to see the photographs and sketches taped to the edge of the painting and pinned on the wall behind: pictures of Julia herself, lying naked on a bed.

As the camera angle pulled back and more of the room came into view, it was clear that this was a studio of some kind: the white walls; the large skylight, angled to give maximum illumination to the room but shaded with muslin against the glare; a glimpse of pictures covering the other wall and a room beyond, dark but for the red glow of a safe-light that had been left on.

'Jake's studio?' Mike questioned.

'It's not the university, and it's certainly not her house or the parents' place.'

'It's worth getting it enhanced,' Mike commented, 'and maybe showing to Max. It's possible he could have been there.'

Peterson nodded but didn't look hopeful. 'He's playing with us again,' he said. 'Showing us so much and none of it's going to be of any use. You just know it.'

'He'll get careless. He has to.'

'I'll be sure and tell him that when we meet.'

Peterson pressed play once more and let the film run. It had changed in character. The same studio, but with Julia dressed only in a green silk robe, standing self-consciously facing Jake. This time they could hear his voice too as he coaxed her into taking off her robe and posing for him: a pleasant, educated voice with the slight twang of a residual accent that Mike could not quite place.

'Come on, Julie darling, I've seen it all before. There's nothing to be shy about.'

'I know, but it's the camera.' She giggled nervously. 'I mean, you might show the film to someone.'

'Why would I do that, darling? Personal consumption this is for. All those long dark nights when you're not around.'

She giggled again. 'And what nights are those?' she asked him. 'I'm here all the time just lately.'

She began to unfasten the belt, biting her lip and looking sideways at him, deliberately provocative as she slid the robe from her shoulders and let it fall to the floor.

'Beautiful,' he said. 'Now move for me, darling, pose a bit, think of it like a life class with a bit of movement.'

She laughed again, posing awkwardly, trying too hard to look sexy and confident, then gradually, as they watched, beginning to relax and play Jake's game.

Her movements became more fluid, more provocative, her eyes on Jake as she touched herself, stroking her own breasts, cupping them in her hands as though presenting them to those watching; her hands moving down onto her belly, and then to the tops of her legs and between her thighs.

Mike swallowed hard, wanting to look away but compelled to go on watching. He felt Peterson shifting uncomfortably in his seat and then get up and cross the room to fill the kettle.

Mike sat still, wishing he'd thought of that first, as Julia Norman played out her role on the screen, totally self-absorbed.

'She's the same age as my youngest,' Peterson commented, his voice gruff with pain and embarrassment.

Mike found himself hoping that Julia's parents had switched off before the tape came to an end.

Chapter Fifteen

Against his usual habits, Jake called in sick on the Thursday morning. Alastair's appearance on the television the night before brought a new twist to the game and he had unfinished business to attend to.

The news that his mother had died so recently had surprised him. He had assumed that she had passed away long ago, or at any rate he had given little thought to her still living.

That morning, Jake had spared his mother an hour of his time, the first he had given her in years.

As the clock in the kitchen ticked away, Jake moved his thoughts to his mother's dying. He wondered what exactly had been wrong with her, how long it had taken her to die and if there had been much pain. He made a mental note that he should ask Alastair when they met.

As the clock began to chime the hour Jake sat very still, waiting for the last of the sounds to fade, then he got up from his seat at the kitchen table, ready to carry on with his day, his thoughts of his mother already as dead and gone as the woman herself.

His father, though, was very much on Jake's mind.

Jake walked out of the kitchen and through the garden. It had rained briefly and the grass was damp, the air still early-morning fresh before the heat of the day. He walked barefoot from the house, relishing the coldness of the rain-soaked grass, filling his lungs with the sharp air. He had searched long and hard to find this little house with its disproportionately large cellar and its view of the ocean. It had been in a terrible state, cheap enough to buy for cash, and he'd spent time and money restoring and rebuilding, doing the work himself at the weekends. He'd converted the attic into a studio and darkroom, having to resort to contractors only to install the three large, north-facing skylight windows that flooded the room with daylight.

At the end of his garden was a rose-hedge and a wooden gate that gave access to the clifftop. The cliff path had once run along here, but coastal erosion had made it dangerous and the path had been diverted for a few hundred yards back onto the narrow road that ran in front of Jake's house and then on through the village. The house, the garden, the location, they all suited Jake: remote enough for privacy, but not so remote that people would be unduly curious. In the village they knew him well, or thought they did: Mr Phillips, the sales rep, not there much because of his job but a really pleasant sort. Always ready to take part in parish events, but a bit quiet like. Not married – they'd heard he was widowed and had never really got over it . . . Gossip always ready to fill a vacuum.

Jake stood on the clifftop looking down onto the ocean as it crashed and raged angrily against the rocks. Even at the height of summer the waves were never still. An undercurrent sent the water churning and writhing against the cliff, no matter how calm the water might be further out or how beautiful the day. It was that which had drawn Jake Bowen here, that above all other things, the sound and sight of the restless water grinding away at the land that supported his garden and his house. The slow relentless pounding that had already claimed the old cliff path would one day swallow all that he now owned.

Jake sat down, oblivious to the cold dampness of the grass, and gazed far out to sea.

Alastair had woken early, his dream still fresh in his mind. He lay in bed, thinking about it, remembering the events that had triggered the image.

He had been walking with his son along the cliff path between Whitby and Robin Hood's Bay. It was a place he had often taken Jake, always being a great one for long, strenuous walks. This time he had something important on his mind.

'I know what you've done,' Alastair Bowen had told his son. 'I know you killed her, Jake.'

Jake made no comment. His father waited, expecting some response, but received none.

'What I don't understand, Jake, what I need to know, is why. Why kill the woman? What had she done to you?'

Jake shrugged. 'Nothing to me,' he said.

'Then why?' Alastair stood still and looked at his son, as though hoping to read something in his face. He shook his head 'You were always evil,' he said. 'That's the only explanation for it. You'll come to a bad end, Jake.'

Jake shrugged again, unconcerned by his father's words. He'd been hearing all his life that he was born the devil's child.

'You think I'm so evil, why don't you turn me in?' he asked.

'You're still my son.'

'Really? I thought my dad had horns and a forked tail, to hear you talk. Nah, you're afraid of what the vicar would say. The pillar of the community with a murderer for a son. You wouldn't like that, would you, daddy dear.'

Alastair's hands clenched spasmodically at his sides. 'It would destroy your mother if she knew,' he said.

'To say nothing of your reputation.'

Jake smiled brightly at his father, his unconcern so blatant. Then, whistling to himself, he walked ahead of Alastair, along the narrow path, head high, daring his father to act.

Jake Bowen was then just fifteen years old.

Thursday had been a quiet and frustrating day. Mike had spent most of it with the collators, assessing results of the door-to-door inquiries. The mammoth effort had begun to verify the identities of everyone who'd stayed in the holiday cottages the year before. So far, nothing of significance had emerged.

There had been the odd sighting of what might have been Jake and Julia, but could just as easily have been a courting couple heading towards the woods. Then there were a few holidaymakers who were proving difficult to trace – people moved house, Mike reminded himself. The sheer volume of information generated when twenty-odd officers went knocking on a lot of doors was staggering. And all of this had to be fitted in with the normal run-of-the-mill summer problems of tourists and petty crime and stolen cars and domestic trouble that went on regardless of the murder inquiry.

Mike glanced up as a police constable came in and spoke his name. The young man looked excited, obviously pleased with himself, and had a worried-looking woman in tow. He ushered her into the room and found her a chair. She sat down automatically. Mike was on the verge of asking what was wrong with using an interview room, but the officer was already talking. 'This lady, sir, she's the one who made the call to Mr Macey.'

'You're certain?'

'Of course, sir. She'll tell you all about it.'

Mike looked sceptically at the woman. She was in her early twenties, he guessed, with dark hair cut short in a very structured style and blue eyes.

'Would you like a cup of tea?' he asked.

'Oh, yes. Yes, I would.' She looked around uncomfortably. 'I've never been in a police station before.'

Mike smiled and gestured to the PC to get the tea, noting with amusement the reluctance with which the young officer stopped hovering and did as he was told. Then he pulled his chair out from behind the desk and moved round to sit on the same side as the young woman, blocking her view of the office activity.

'I'm Inspector Mike Croft,' he said. 'I'm going to have to ask you to make a formal statement in a minute, but for now if you'd like to just tell me about the phone call, Miss . . .?'

'Watson. Liv – that's short for Olivia – Watson.' Her voice was a little slurred, as though she had started drinking early. She grinned suddenly, nervously. 'Aren't I supposed to ask for a lawyer or something?'

Mike smiled back. 'Not unless I arrest you.'

'You think you might?'

'No. No, I don't think so.' Mike leaned back in his chair, aware that he was being flirted with and a little flattered. 'You wanted to tell me about the phone call Miss Watson.'

'Call me Liv.' She grinned at him again, wrinkling her nose. She had freckles, he noticed, spreading across onto her cheeks.

'Liv,' he said obediently. 'The call?'

She sighed elaborately. 'To Mr Ed Macey, at the paper in Dorchester. There was this man, you see. We'd all been talking to him a few nights before.'

'We?'

'Me and some friends. We'd had a few to drink and this guy, he was chatting to us at the bar. Oh, thanks,' she said, as the PC brought the tea, setting it carefully on the table and then hovering in the background once again.

'Go on,' Mike said.

'Well, Linda, that's one of my friends, she'd got into a row with her boyfriend and gone storming off outside.'

'This was the day you made the phone call?'

'No. No, I told you, this was, I don't know, about three nights before. Linda will remember. She had a row with her boyfriend, like I said, so she's bound to re-member when it was, you see?'

Mike nodded patiently, wishing he'd handed her straight on to someone else.

'And this man talked to you?'

'Yeah, he was friendly, you know. Not too flirty but nice. Good-looking too. You'll want a description?'

'You can give it to this officer here, when you make your statement.'

'Oh.' For a moment she sounded disappointed. 'OK, then.' She brightened, switching her attention to the younger man.

'You were telling me about the phone call.'

'Yeah, but you see he'd been there that night.'

'When Linda and her boyfriend had the row?'

'Yeah, and he stopped Linda from storming out, said it wasn't safe and she should at least let him call a taxi for her.'

'And did he?' Mike asked.

'No, Linda's boyfriend got jealous then, said if anyone was going to call a taxi it should be him, and it looked as though it was going to get really nasty. Like I told you, we'd all had a lot to drink.' She smiled up at the young PC. 'Then we saw him again that lunch-time. He'd spent ages smoothing things over with Linda and her fellah, so we got talking.'

'It didn't turn nasty then?'

'Oh, no, he was a real fast talker. We all ended up having a drink together.' She frowned. 'I can't remember when he left, but I think it was close to chucking-out time. Anyway, this lunch-time, we were all having a drink. We're all on holiday, you see, so it doesn't matter. I mean, we don't drink at lunch-time when we're at work.' She paused, waiting.

'I'm sure you don't.'

'And we were all saying how good he'd been the other night, helping Linda get back with her boyfriend and smoothing over the row, and he said, if we were so grateful, would I help him play a joke on a friend. It was a surprise or something. So I said yeah, why not?'

'And he dialled the paper and you took over after he got past the switchboard?'

She nodded. 'I was supposed to make the call, but – ' she giggled – 'I'd had a bit to drink and I couldn't keep the number in my head.'

'You managed to remember the message.'

'Oh, that. He'd written it down, but I kept having to ask him if I'd got it right.'

Mike nodded thoughtfully. 'And you've not seen him since?'

'No, but he said he was on holiday down here, visiting friends or something, so I supposed he'd gone home.' She frowned suddenly. 'Nobody's told me what this is all about,' she said. 'Just that they were looking for someone who might have made a call for someone else to Mr Macey. It was the name I remembered. Mr Ed Macey, who writes for the paper.' She stared hard at Mike. 'It's about that murder, isn't it? Something to do with the murder.'

'Drink your tea,' Mike told her, 'and then if you could go with this young man here and make a formal statement. You've been very helpful, Liv.'

'It *is* to do with the murder,' she shouted. 'I knew it. I just knew it. I told Linda, this is all about that dead girl.' She stood up suddenly, nervous excitement aided by lunch-time alcohol, looking around as though the murderer might be hiding in the room. 'I want police protection,' she demanded. 'I'm not going to wait until he decides to come back. I want police protection.'

Mike sighed, he'd been surprised she'd not made the connection before, but he'd figured that the alcohol might have softened her perceptions.

'We'll arrange for someone to give you a lift home,' he told her, 'and give you some general advice. Or maybe you'd like to stay with a friend for a few days? But really, Miss Watson, I don't think you have anything to worry about.'

She was still protesting as she was led away to make her statement, the PC giving Mike a look that spoke volumes about his opinion of Mike's protective instincts.

Mike shrugged. The young man was still a probationer and had a lot to learn. He was amused to hear him promise the girl that he'd personally arrange for an eye to be kept on her. In fact, he'd attend to it himself.

Mike smiled. Well, the girl *was* pretty.

Interesting, though, the way Jake had made two very public appearances like that. How carefully had he planned that side of it? Had he worried in case Macey taped his calls? If so, that didn't explain his voice on the video tape of Julia Norman. It would be interesting, too, to see what Jake had chosen to look like this time.

*

Jo had awoken screaming, her sedative-induced sleep producing nightmares in which Essie called for her, shouting and pleading for help. Her screams woke the entire household and started the new baby crying.

Maria glanced at the clock on Jo's bedside table. It was one thirty, they had been asleep maybe less than an hour.

Jo's mother and husband were there to comfort her and Maria was surplus to requirements. She picked up the crying baby and cuddled him close, carrying him downstairs and away from all the noise. He was unlikely to settle again until he'd been fed, she decided. Jo left bottles made up in the fridge that just needed warming. She could see to that.

Maria let the baby moan in his cradle chair while she filled the kettle and got the bottle from the fridge. Rocked him gently, chatting to him while the kettle boiled, then stood the bottle in a jug of boiling water to warm through and boiled the kettle again for tea.

From upstairs she could hear Jo, still crying for her lost child, this new one forgotten in her grief. Jo had barely been able to bring herself to hold her little boy in the days since Essie had gone. She had seen every gesture of affection towards her son as a betrayal of her love for Essie. Maria had taken over, glad of something that she could do without seeming in her turn to be forgetting about the missing child.

Maria checked the bottle and then picked up the baby, carrying him around the kitchen as he fed hungrily. She glanced out through the half-open kitchen curtain. The police car was still parked at the front of the house, two figures inside dimly silhouetted. They had offered to take Jo and her family to a safe house or to stay with friends. Somewhere private, when media interest threatened to take over and journalists seemed ready to camp outside their door.

Jo had refused, terrified that the kidnapper might phone and she would not be there to take the call. No one could persuade her otherwise, so they had simply closed the curtains and existed since the Monday night in a twilight world. It had been a relief when, after a couple of days of inaction, the press and television had retreated to camp out in the bar of a local hotel.

The curtains, though, had still remained closed as if the family already mourned.

The baby had fallen asleep in her arms. She put him back in his cradle chair and covered him with a blanket. Poor little thing, she thought, he didn't even have a name yet and no one had gotten around to registering his birth. She must ask Jo if she should do it in the morning, trying to remember if it had to be a parent who did it. She was vaguely surprised that she didn't know.

Maria poured the tea and took a tray upstairs. Jo's husband thanked her. The two women still wept softly, sitting on the bed, May's arms around Jo.

Then Maria retreated once more to the kitchen. She had felt such guilt at having taken Essie with her to see Mike, though common sense told her that, as Essie had been abducted from so close to her own home, Jake Bowen would have traced the child no matter what. Jo blamed her, though, and while she could understand her sister feeling that way, it hurt terribly.

She fished the mobile phone out of her bag and hesitated for a moment before dialling Mike's number. It was after two in the morning and there was no reason he should have his mobile switched on, never mind be pleased at being disturbed, but she needed to talk to him, to hear a friendly voice. He answered on the third ring, sleepy and surprised.

'Sorry I woke you,' she said, instinctively keeping her voice low, even though it was unlikely anyone would hear her from upstairs.

'I'm not,' he said. 'I went to sleep thinking about you. You must have heard me.'

She laughed. 'Maybe I did. How are you?'

'Frustrated.'

She laughed again, then covered her mouth with her hand, in case Jo might hear. It seemed so long since anyone had made her laugh, it was a relief to know that she still could.

'Any news?' Mike asked her.

'Nothing. God, Mike, it's the not knowing that's so hard. Why doesn't he get in touch?'

'I don't know,' he told her. 'If any of us understood Jake Bowen, we might be a lot further on towards bringing him in.'

'What about your famous psychologists?'

'Can't agree between themselves. Oh, I don't mean to insult them, love, but this time they seem as foxed as any of us.'

'And the father, is he any use?'

'Not a lot so far, but I'm hoping.' He paused. 'Look, we're both on mobiles, I'm not keen on saying too much.'

'I'm sorry, I should have thought.'

She didn't speak for a little while.

Mike said, 'Are you still there?'

'Yes. Yes, of course I am. I'm sorry. My head's so full of all this, it's hard to talk about anything else.'

'I know. It must be. Look, give me a time tomorrow, use a call box if you have to, and I'll ring back.'

Two o'clock, she told him, and then the renewed crying of the baby ending her time of peace.

Jake too had woken from a troubled sleep, but there was nothing unusual in that. He had never been one who needed his eight hours a night; he'd been an insomniac all his life, even as a child getting up at all hours and prowling around the house, enjoying his solitary ownership of it while his parents slept.

He went to look at Essie. She was sleeping but restless and he lifted her, supporting her shoulders as he gave her a drink. She looked up at him with drugged eyes that betrayed no comprehension of who he was or what was happening to her. She had wet herself, too deeply sedated to have bladder control.

Jake brought fresh towels and lay the child on them, taking the soiled ones and putting them into the washing machine. He brought soap and water and washed the small body, drying her carefully. Then he fetched his camera and shot another few minutes of film. The child was so small, he thought, and had such a fragile hold on life. He came close enough to watch her breathing, the rise and fall of the tiny ribcage. He imagined her heart beating, slightly faster each time she breathed in, slightly slower on the out-breath, a pendulum that swung a little too far one way, unable to find a balanced centre.

He sat back on his heels, watching her with naked eyes, the camera put aside, and remembered being five years old and the feel of his fathers hand tight around his wrists: one large hand to hold onto both of his. He remembered the sound of his father's belt being pulled from its loops, the sussussing sound as he tugged it free, and later that day, Jake recalled, he had watched from the window of his room as his father went out into the shadowed yard at the back of their house. There was a raised bed at one end of the concrete surfaced yard that Jake's mother had made with bricks and earth and planted with roses. Jake watched as Alastair dug a deep hole beside a yellow rose and planted what remained of the dead cat inside.

Jake could still taste the salty tang of blood in his mouth.

Chapter Sixteen

Jake had three national papers delivered daily and was gratified to see that he figured in all of them. Macey's interview with Charlie Morrow, due out that day, had been sold on to a news agency and picked up by two out of the three dailies that Jake read. The two tabloids led with the story and with pictures of Charlie Morrow, his face turned so that the scarring showed to best effect. The broadsheet had the story as a front-page feature, but what it led with, and what on closer inspection the tabloids had caught onto, was what Jake had really been waiting for. Someone had made the Jake–Essie connection. In less than five days and without the little clue he'd left them.

Jake was impressed.

A closer reading told him that it was Macey himself who had identified Essie as the niece of Dr Maria Lucas, the woman Mike Croft had been dating for the past two years. Their pictures appeared on page three of both of the tabloids, one featuring them next to its daily nude. Jake couldn't help comparing the two women, dwelling on what Maria Lucas might look like displayed on page three. What would DI Croft think to that?

If he could find the right head shot, Jake thought, from those he had taken that weekend at Lyme, then it would be no trouble to arrange it. He had enough black female nudes in his reference collection to make it easy, and all the right software.

Daydreaming about selling a remodelled Maria Lucas to the *Sun*, he set about getting his breakfast. He had already fed Essie some milk and changed the towels again. He still had not decided what to do with her. He'd taken some still shots of her that morning, not particularly provocative but good enough to fetch a reasonable price, especially as the morning news meant he'd have no trouble establishing provenance.

Jake poured his morning tea and stood looking out of the window at the promise of a bright new day. The sky was a polished blue and the sun already glared off the glimpse of sea on the horizon.

What really gave Jake the best buzz was to think of all the effort that was being put into catching him, when every day he was out and about, available, dealing with the public: asking policemen for directions; chatting to people in the street, interacting with them, touching them, liking them and being liked in return. He even formed brief relationships with some of them, relationships of the sweetest and most loving kind. And none of them ever suspected a thing – until it was too late.

He thought of Julia, poor repressed little Julia, so flattered by all his attention and concern. Mummy and Daddy not really understanding the artistic temperament and, to be fair, Julia not wanting them to let go too fast.

She'd been shy, found working in the shared studio at the university so very hard, and when Jake had offered her a place to paint she had jumped at it.

'Don't say anything though,' he'd warned her, as their

relationship swiftly became more and more intense. 'I'm supposed to agree not to get involved with the students. My company goes overboard on corporate image and if they found I was sleeping with one of my customers' young ladies that might be the end of my job.'

Jake had never been certain whether she believed him completely, but she liked the idea of a secret lover – so romantic – especially one who took her away for expensive weekends and provided a place to work and materials that she could never afford on a student loan.

He'd let her have Christmas with her family, deliver her painting, and enjoyed imagining their confusion and concern when they studied the subject matter. He knew they were far too polite and well bred to say anything to Julia.

He'd brought her back to the house after the Christmas break and told her there was something he wanted to show her in the basement. She had never left it again until the day she died, though he'd let her have her books and drawing things.

Poor Julia, she'd had a lot of talent.

Jake turned back to the table and flicked the paper over to the front page, staring hard at the images of Charlie Morrow.

Jake approved of talent and knew that he had plenty. He took scissors from the kitchen drawer and clipped the pictures of Charlie from the paper, then took them up to his studio and pinned them to the wall, wondering as he did so just how far the burns were likely to extend.

'A real Jake Bowen original,' he said.

*

Peterson stormed into the incident room at Honiton and threw the stack of morning papers onto Mike's desk.

Mike moved them off the report he had been reading. 'I've already seen them,' he said.

Peterson sat down. 'Our superiors are not happy,' he said.

'Perhaps if they're so superior they could have told us how to avoid it,' Mike said. 'Someone was bound to make the connection some time and, frankly, I don't see it's done us any good sitting on it. We're still no nearer finding the child.'

Peterson gave him a suspicious look. 'Mike, if I thought you or Maria had anything to do with leaking this, you'd be off this case quicker than I could say Jack Crap.'

'If I'd known that, I'd have leaked it sooner,' Mike said wryly. 'Oh, come off it, we may as well bow to the inevitable. I told Ed Macey nothing. He must have made his own connections.'

'Sometimes, Mike, I wonder about your attitude.'

'Sometimes, so do I.'

Peterson didn't reply to this but stood up again. 'I've got to go,' he said. 'Trouble at home.'

'Oh.'

'My daughter's place. It was broken into. She's been away since those damned pictures arrived so no one's quite sure when.'

'Wasn't the place alarmed?' Mike asked.

'They're out in the middle of nowhere. People don't even lock their bloody doors.' He sighed. 'Yes, it was alarmed. She was upset, thinks she forgot to set it on

Monday when they went to get their things. I said I'd go and see what was missing then get back to her. She doesn't want to go herself. She's terrified about going home, Mike. Scared out of her wits.'

Mike nodded. 'I can understand that.'

'Meantime,' Peterson said, 'you'd better go and see our friend Macey. Oh, and we're going ahead with the *Crimewatch* thing. The voice enhancement from that video tape should be ready by then. Maybe the bastard overstepped himself this time.'

'I hope so,' Mike said quietly.

After Peterson had left, Mike went back to what he had been doing, trying to get clear in his mind the various strands of the Bowen inquiry. So many people tied up all over the country by one man. So much information and so little of it that connected or made any obvious sense.

He'd been looking again at the descriptions of Jake that had surfaced. Liv Watson and her friends had him as a man with sandy-coloured hair and pale blue eyes. Freckled skin, they said, and about six feet tall.

The man seen leaving Caldwell's house at the time he must have died was dark, with a beard, and Max Harriman swore that Jake had wavy brown hair and grey-green eyes. He gave Jake's height as being a shade under six feet. That, at least, was vaguely consistent.

There were other sightings, all of them variable, some of them recorded by police artists or computer-generated images, even old-fashioned photofit. There was little match barring Jake's height and his weight – well built and definitely not fat, not even around the middle, as Liv had commented in her statement.

Alastair had confirmed that his son had grey-green eyes and light brown hair, but contacts can be worn and hair coloured, and wigs and false beards no longer had to look as if they'd fallen out of Christmas crackers.

Mike looked at the dozen random images set out on the desk and tried to fit together some kind of composite – the essential Jake that remained even behind the masks he wore.

He picked up the final image as Alastair Bowen came through the door. The picture of Jake at fifteen had been scanned into a computer and aged to give a simulation of how he might be now: Jake at nearly forty derived from Jake as a teenage boy. Mike wondered just how accurate this was ever going to be.

He pushed the images across to Alastair, who regarded them solemnly. Alastair's own features and those of his wife, taken from a photograph of them both close to Jake's present age, had been added to the mix and the artist and programmer who had worked upon it professed to be very pleased with the result.

'You think he looks like this?' Alastair mused.

'I don't think anything any more. I've discovered it's a waste of time.'

Alastair glanced up at him and laughed shortly, then looked back at the picture. 'Handsome,' he said. 'Not flashy, but a good-looking man.'

Mike nodded. 'That comes over in all the descriptions,' he said. 'And he looks younger than thirty-nine. No one placed him older than mid-thirties, most ten years younger than we know he is.'

It was a sharply featured profile. Slightly prominent

nose, high cheekbones and a squarish jaw with a small cleft in the chin. The eyes were large and widely set, with heavy but well-shaped brows. Looking at Alastair, Mike could see a definite resemblance. Alastair was a man in his late sixties and the face had become slack with age and two years of worry about his wife, but it was still a challenging face, the eyes intelligent and alert.

Alastair pulled another picture towards him, the one of Jake at fifteen years old. Clutching the super eight camera, the teacher who had helped him with his film-making standing behind him and Max Harriman at his side, grinning at the camera.

'This teacher, Mr Wright,' Mike said. 'How close was Jake to him?'

Alastair thought before replying. 'Jake used him the same as he used everyone,' he said, 'but the teacher didn't know that. He believed in Jake, thought he had a great future, and I think Jake respected him. He went to his funeral at least.'

'He died in a car accident,' Mike reminded himself.

'That's right. Not long after Jake won the prize for making the film. Jake actually cried at the funeral.' He shook his head, disbelieving. 'The family were so impressed by that. It meant so much that their father and husband had made a difference. It was all sham, of course, but they didn't know that.'

'The film,' Mike said, 'tell me about it.'

'I can't tell you much more than the paper did,' he said, referring to the article that accompanied the photograph. 'There was a strike, a big, long-term strike at one of the local factories. We're talking the time of the recession and the three-day week. You remember that?'

Mike nodded.

'Like having the Victorian times back again. Oil lamps in the blackouts and candles selling out in all the shops. I remember the kids running about the streets with flashlights and all the parents yelling at them not to waste the batteries.'

Mike smiled. He'd been only a kid at the time too. For him it had meant missing school because the heating didn't work and half the time there was no power.

'The strike?' he reminded Alastair.

'Ah, yes. It was at a local pit. When we still had such animals as coal mines back home. They'd been on the three-day week, like all the rest of us, short of cash, and, believe me, where we lived everyone was short enough without adding to it. It was a crazy time to call everyone out, but they did it. I forget the reasons behind it. Showing solidarity or some such, as I recall, but it fascinated Jake. He went round interviewing management, strikers, pickets, anyone that would talk to him. Went into their houses, showing how hard up they were and how much they must have believed in what they were doing if they were putting their whole livelihood at risk by acting like this. Saw himself as a proper documentary film-maker.'

'And Max, what was his part in this?'

'Max just tagged along so far as I could see. Carried stuff. I think he helped with the editing, but I don't know much more than that really. Max idolized Jake. I don't think he needed to do much to be happy, it was enough just to be there.'

'And yet Jake allowed him to take equal credit.'

Alastair shrugged. 'Who knows?' he said. 'Who knows why Jake does anything? Maybe the teacher made him give Max credit. I don't remember, Inspector. It was a long time ago.'

Mike nodded and was about to speak again when someone called him from across the room. He excused himself and left Alastair to his thoughts.

That had been a strange, eventful period. Alastair himself had been on short time. By then he was working in a hardware store and the pay was average at best. He was looking forward to Jake leaving school that summer so he could at least contribute to household expenses, but the teachers wanted him to stay on. Alastair had not been happy. The idea of another two years supporting his son was not something he relished. Already Jake worked four nights a week in the local chip shop, keeping late hours as they stayed open to catch workers coming off the closing shift, though even they had been affected by the three-day week. But Alastair couldn't see the point in him staying on at school any longer. Just what did Jake plan on doing with his life anyway?

Jake had loved that winter. No streetlights, walking home in the pitch black or through streets lit on one side while the other showed only candlelight through the curtains. Alastair had never been able to work out the way the power zones worked. Why, for example, their neighbours three doors down had power when they did not or vice versa. It had been a fine time for Jake,

the streets around their home almost deserted and no
one to watch what he did or where he went.

Alastair frowned. He needed to talk to Max again.

Peterson had arrived at his daughter's house accompanied
by two local officers.

'As you can see, sir, the back door's been forced, but
it was only when it blew open that anyone noticed.
Your daughter asked the postman to give her letters to a
neighbour but didn't leave the keys with anyone to switch
lights on or anything.'

'She had a lot on her mind,' Peterson commented.

The officer nodded. 'If you'd take a look around, sir,
but nothing's been disturbed as far as we can tell and
there's nothing obvious missing.'

Peterson walked slowly through his daughter's house.
The children's rooms, filled with their toys, the youngest's
bed still unmade. The room his daughter and her
husband shared, bed made, everything tidy but for a shirt
sticking out of the laundry bin in the en suite shower
room.

Downstairs, everything looked normal. As tidy as a
house could be with three children in it. TV and VCR
still in their place. Stack system and CDs on the shelf in
the corner. Nothing missing as far as he could see.

In the kitchen, an unwashed mug sat in the sink,
traces of lipstick on the rim. Other breakfast pots,
washed and in the drainer. His daughter, Peterson remembered, had always been very organized. It was no real
surprise that she would have everything done before she

had to take the children to school. The post had arrived, she'd said, just before she'd been about to leave. She'd opened the mail, seen the pictures and left for his house.

Everything done, except for that unmade bed . . .

Peterson turned to one of the officers. 'When's SOCO due to arrive?'

'Probably not until tomorrow, otherwise it'll be Monday.'

Peterson nodded. Like many scenes of crime units, this one was now civilian-run. They'd have to come out from Bristol and, with there being nothing missing and his daughter not being here, this would not have been graded as priority.

'I just want to look at something again.'

He beckoned to the officer and led him back upstairs to the room shared by the youngest children. The smallest one had her bed under the window. It was stacked with teddies, all neatly arranged at the end and the bed covered with a Barbie quilt and pillow. The quilt was pulled back, whereas all the other beds were neatly made.

Peterson eased the quilt back a little further. In the middle of the bed, decorated with blue and yellow beads, lay one of Essie's braids.

Chapter Seventeen

Macey was ecstatic. He sat with the stack of nationals in front of him, explaining to Liz and anyone else who would listen that this was definitely *it*: Macey had finally made it big. Liz, having pored over the copy he'd pushed under her nose and done her best to congratulate him effusively enough, wanted to move on, but Macey, despite his worldly wise, done-it-all air, was like a sponge, in need of constant praise.

'How's Charlie getting along, anyway?' Liz asked him.

'We'll find out later on today,' Macey said. 'I tried to call him this morning but he was having his physio or something. Those hands.' Macey shuddered elaborately.

Liz cast him an amused glance. 'I like him,' she said. Macey nodded agreement before looking up sharply. 'Knew it would only be a matter of time,' he said, then more loudly, 'Inspector Croft, nice to see you again this morning.'

Mike didn't bother replying. He grabbed a chair from a nearby desk and sat down, leaning forward to study Macey's newspapers.

'How did you know?' he asked.

'Saw your lady on the TV appeal and recognized her,' Macey said. He reached into his desk and pulled out a folder of clippings, found the one he wanted and gave it to Mike. A local journalist had caught them both on camera during an earlier case Mike had worked on in Norwich. Maria had been professionally involved with a woman suspect. Mike had forgotten that this particular picture even existed.

'There are others,' Macey said. 'Things your lady's been involved in and dragged you along to. Some sort of charity ball, I think one of them is. You look nice in a dinner jacket. Want me to find it?'

Mike shook his head. 'I'll pass,' he said. 'And you didn't think of the consequences, that we might not want this information released?'

'Oh, you're asking me so nicely, Inspector. It makes me nervous. Is the bad cop waiting round the corner?'

Liz glared at Macey, before asking Mike anxiously, 'You think it will make things worse?'

Mike shook his head slowly. 'I doubt it will make much difference,' he said. 'Not to Essie or to Jake. To the family, though, now that it's publicly confirmed Jake Bowen has their child, I don't imagine it's going to be easy for them.'

'Or for you,' Macey said. 'How does it feel to know she was taken because of you, Inspector Croft? That this little girl has been kidnapped by a psychopath because you're dating her auntie?'

'Macey!' Liz was outraged, but Mike was wearied beyond retaliating. It was something he'd been charging himself with every hour since Essie disappeared.

'How do you think it feels, Mr Macey?' Mike said softly. 'If I could trade places with her, then you can be certain that I would.'

He got up then and walked slowly back towards the door.

'He didn't deserve that, Ed,' Liz told him angrily.

Macey threw her an apologetic look. It lasted all of a second and she almost missed it.

'Can I quote you on that, Inspector Croft?' he shouted at Mike's retreating back.

Peterson was back at Honiton by the time Mike got there. Mike had driven slowly along the Dorchester road, allowing cars to rush past him on the dual carriageway and vaguely aware of impatient drivers behind him when the road narrowed for the villages.

He didn't care. Macey's words had bitten all the harder for being true. He should have come back at him, Mike thought, told him what he really thought of someone who could expose his guilt so openly, but Mike knew he'd only have regretted it. He'd done his best to stay professional and calm, knowing Macey was merely being Macey, riding high upon the moment and made brave by success.

He would, though, do anything to know that Essie was safe once more. Would, as he had told Macey, willingly have traded places with her. He wondered if Macey would print his parting comment and how he himself would have to respond if Macey did; and if, in some half-conscious way, he had been hoping to use Macey to deliver a message to Bowen.

His despairing mood was not lifted as he drove back into Honiton.

Police were still doing the last of the house-to-house calls, with extra officers drafted in from wherever they could be spared. The incident room was full to overflowing, desks crammed in wherever they could be fitted. Notice boards and stacks of paper vied for space with empty cans and sandwich bags.

Peterson waved him over as soon as he came through the door.

'I need a couple of hours, Mike. If anyone asks, you can't raise me. My battery's flat in the mobile or something.'

'What's wrong?'

'I'm getting my family out, Mike. I just need a couple of hours to make arrangements.'

'Certainly, but out where?'

Peterson shook his head. 'I'm sorry, Mike, I'm not telling even you. I'll be leaving something with my bank, saying where they can be reached should anything happen to me, but I'm telling no one else.'

Mike had never seen Peterson so rattled. 'What did you find at the house?' he said.

Peterson led him over to where the evidence was being filed and pulled from the box the bag containing Essie's hair.

'This was on my granddaughter's bed.'

Charlie Morrow had come back from the morning's physio and logged on again. He'd spent several hours so far sitting on the side and monitoring various of the user groups that Macey had directed him to. The thing that had struck him most was the banality of it all. The 'public rooms', to which he had easiest access, were places to exchange gossip; to shock the unwary and enjoy the mild frisson of discussing sexual practices, both regular and somewhat dubious, with the illusion of complete freedom.

Talk had turned to Jake from time to time. The film-maker was something of a legend, even though, on closer inquiry, it turned out that no one in the public rooms could honestly say they had seen one of his films. They were, in the main, collectors' items, expensive and exclusive.

Jake Bowen had started out in soft porn and his early work was being re-released now that he'd hit the headlines. 'He's an artist,' someone said, implying that artists were allowed to cross the line between good and bad taste; explore the difference between life and death and the full range of sexual experience.

Charlie doubted any of them really knew what they were talking about. Jake was not some esoteric film-maker, exploring the links between a good fuck and a fear of dying. He realized quickly that of all those he encountered in the user groups, he was likely to be the only one who had actually seen one of Jake Bowen's special editions.

The beautifully shot and cruelly erotic images still lived in his mind and haunted his dreams.

He wondered if Jake would contact him; if Jake would be as curious about Charlie Morrow as Charlie was about Jake and, if he was, how he would choose to make contact. He decided to make another opening for Jake, just in case.

He picked at random a half dozen of the sites and left a message on each, varying the suggested meeting time by five minutes.

The message read: 'Meet me at eleven p.m. Regards, Charlie.'

Maria phoned Mike just after two o'clock. She was using a public phone and he called her back.

'How are you?' he asked.

'Pleased to be out. Someone had to shop.'

'You've seen the papers today?'

'I've seen the journalists. Most of them are camped outside Jo's front door. I went out over the wall and through a neighbour's garden. I think Jo's about to cave in and agree to move out for a few days.'

'Where will she go? Will you go with her?'

'We've relatives in Kent, that seems favourite at the moment, but no, I don't think I'll be going. I have to get back to Oaklands.'

'Not to work, surely?'

'Not with patients, no. I've off-loaded my urgent cases as best I can but there's always something to do. I've a backlog of paperwork like you wouldn't believe.'

'At least I'll be able to talk to you there.'

'There is that.' She paused. She'd been giving things a lot of thought, particularly Alastair Bowen. 'How are you getting along with the father?'

Alastair was across the other side of the room, talking

to another officer. 'Slowly,' Mike said. 'He's got a lot to tell, but it's hard work.'

Maria took a deep breath. 'You think he'll talk to me?'

'To you? I don't know. I don't know if Peterson would even agree.'

'Suppose he did, would Alastair?'

'He hates shrinks, won't have anything to do with ours. We were hoping he'd work with the forensic psychologists, but he won't even entertain the idea.'

'Can't you force him?'

'How? Torture went out with the Inquisition.'

'Very funny. Look, can't you at least ask him? Not as a shrink but because of Essie. You say he came forward because he heard about Essie?'

'So he claims. Look, frankly I take everything he says with a large pinch of salt.'

He thought about it for a moment, watching Alastair from across the room. Maria might be able to get through in a way that he could not.

'I'll talk to him,' he said. 'That's all I can promise.'

Alastair Bowen was not at first amenable to Mike's request.

'She's not asking as a psychiatrist,' Mike said, 'but simply because of Essie.'

'I didn't think personal involvement was allowed.'

Mike sighed. 'You're involved,' he pointed out.

'Hardly the same thing though, is it?'

He fell silent then and Mike decided to wait him

out. He went to fetch coffee for them both from the machine in the front office. On his return Alastair began to speak.

'I took Jake to see a counsellor,' he said. 'We paid for it. I thought I should at least give him a chance.'

'What made you think he needed help?' he asked.

Alastair frowned. 'His mother thought there was something wrong,' he said. He sipped his coffee slowly, pausing to stare into the polystyrene cup as though it might give him inspiration. 'Jake was always a bit of a loner, I suppose. Didn't play with other kids unless you forced him to. He was always different. I knew it would only be a matter of time before his mother realized something wasn't right, but I couldn't tell her what it was. Not what it really was.'

Mike made no comment, not certain he wanted to provoke another of Alastair's statements that Jake had been born the way he was.

Alastair was not to be put off by a little silence.

'I know you don't believe me, Inspector Croft,' he said, 'but you had to be there to understand. See what Jake did to people, to . . . animals. To his toys even. You had to be there to understand, and in the end it was obvious to me. I hadn't been imagining things. That look *was* there right from the time that Jake was born. That look of pure evil, wrapped up in charm.'

'Perhaps,' Mike ventured, 'hearing you say it so often . . .'

'Made him that way? No, I've told you before. I did my best for the boy, tried all I knew to save him, but none of it would work. Then he kept getting into fights at school and the teachers started poking around about how he was at home – was he happy? Was he having problems? – and his mother decided maybe they were right. The loving little boy she'd always convinced herself he was, was showing his true colours and she didn't know what to do.'

'How old was Jake?' Mike asked.

'Just turned thirteen,' Alastair said.

Mike waited, to see if Alastair was about to find significance in the age, but he made no comment on it. Instead, he went on, 'You can imagine, we kept it pretty quiet. I mean, the background we came from, no one "went into therapy" or whatever the jargon is today. They'd have laughed themselves stupid, those neighbours of ours. But I did it for my wife and she did it for Jake. It was this young woman, the therapist. Fresh out of college from the look of her. Green as grass. She was no match for Jake. He refused to cooperate for weeks, and I was all set to give up, but his mother reckoned he was getting in less trouble at school and it must be working. So we carried on. He didn't talk to her, not for all that time, then, suddenly, he poured out his soul to the stupid woman. Talking about all the abuse and cruelty he'd suffered. Blamed me for everything.'

'You admitted to having beaten him,' Mike said quietly.

Alastair's eyes flashed with a sudden anger. 'And I make no apology for it,' he said.

'She called in the social worker. Got the police involved. We managed to keep it quiet, but it almost got to the courts. Then two days before we were due to appear, he laughed in her face and told her it was all lies. Told her how much of a fool she was.'

'And she believed him?' Mike asked.

Alastair shrugged. 'The police carried on poking around for a while, but then the case was dropped. It was only his word and he'd gone back on that.'

'But there was some truth in what he'd said,' Mike persisted. 'Did you make him retract his statement?'

Alastair Bowen refused to reply, fixing Mike with an icy stare.

Mike leaned across the table towards him. 'Talk to Maria,' he said, hating the desperation he could not keep out of his voice. 'Talk to her about Jake. How it all began. Anything you might know that will help us to save Essie.' Memories of the time he'd spent with them, at Lyme and on other family occasions, flooded back. Mike pushed himself away from the table, got up and walked over to the window, staring blindly at the bright, sunlit world outside.

'She's probably already dead,' Alastair said softly, 'you know that, don't you?'

Mike turned angrily and crossed back to where Alastair was still seated, all pretence at professional calm gone.

'And that's what I'm supposed to tell the family?' he said. 'Is that all you have to say? I'm not going to give up, none of us are. You want us to write this off and wait around till there are other Essies? Other Julia Normans? Other children? I know what it is to lose a child, Alastair.'

'So do I, Inspector Croft,' Alastair said heavily. He sat forward with his head in his hands. 'So do I.'

Jake had decided that the focus of his attention from now on should be Mike Croft, as he was the one most in contact with Alastair. He needed to find a way of getting Alastair alone and Inspector Croft looked most likely to be the one to show him how.

He went down to the basement, gave Essie milk and washed her, changing the wet towels she was lying on. He sat for a while watching the child. She moved restlessly in her sleep, her flickering eyes telling him that she dreamed.

Jake pulled the child to him and held her in his arms, cradling her gently. Her skin was so very, very soft and he had washed her with perfumed soap, the scent clinging to her as he brought his head close.

'Does your mummy love you, little girl? Does she play with you and cuddle you and tell you how special you are?' He smiled suddenly. 'I know your auntie does,' he told her. 'And your Uncle Mike.'

Chapter Eighteen

Saturday arrived with unexpected rain. It was just over a week since Julia's body had been found and a week exactly since Mike had met with Maria and Essie at Lyme. He'd returned to the woods above Colwell Barton, the murder site still cordoned off and the entrance to that part of the woods barred.

The trees grew thickly enough to shelter him from the worst of the rain and the rhythmic beating of it falling on the canopy of leaves was soothing.

He'd gone into the office early to catch up with some of the reports he'd not had time to read and would not have time to look at later. Most of his day about to be taken up with the return match between Max Harriman and Alastair Bowen.

They'd had a more complete set of toxicology results on Julia Norman's body. They confirmed the high level of amphetamine that early results had suggested and also a residual amount of barbiturates. The guess was that Julia had been kept sedated for quite some time, then pumped full of uppers, enough to compensate for the weakness brought on by blood loss. She'd have been high enough to fly when Jake brought her to the woods, then at some point she'd been hit from behind, just beside the left ear, hard enough to put her down. Then Jake had finished the killing of Julia Norman.

The blood loss had been a difficult thing to account for. Had she lost too much at once, the experts said, the body would have gone into shock and she might well have died sooner. Jake must have taken things slowly, Mike thought; watched Julia dying over many days before bringing her here. It was that element of calculation that he found so sickening.

He stood just outside the inner cordon surrounding the small altar on which Julia had lain. The flowers were completely withered and many had gone. Despite the officer on guard on the main path, souvenir hunters had been here, finding their way into the woods from across the fields, taking the flowers.

Yet other people had come into the woods to lay wreathes or light candles, as Jake himself had done.

There was no stopping them, short of increasing the guard, and with manpower stretched to breaking point on the rest of the inquiry that was impossible.

Mike glanced at his watch. He would have to collect Alastair soon. It was so still and silent here in this part of the woods: only the sound of falling rain and the occasional fizz as heavier drops forced their way through and hit the dust on the forest floor. It was not a comfortable place to be.

Mike glanced around. The creeping feeling between his shoulder blades, as though someone was watching him from the shadows, refused to go away. Jake had observed Macey in the woods that day; watched him and captured his reaction on film. Mike wondered how many times he himself had been the subject of similar Jake Bowen attention.

He turned away and scrambled over the fallen trees, climbing back towards the path.

After his talk with Alastair the day before, he'd sent for whatever records had been kept from when Jake had been thirteen and ready to accuse his father. Mike was not sure what to make of all that. Alastair was clearly convinced that his son was evil incarnate, but what had come first? Had Jake given Alastair cause for doubt right from babyhood – something Mike, remembering the adoration he had felt for his own baby son, found hard to believe. Or was it that Jake's actions had so impressed themselves upon his father's memories that Alastair could simply not remember the time before.

He must speak to Charlie Morrow later, he reminded himself. The *Crimewatch* special on the Jake Bowen case was scheduled for Tuesday and, following the recent media publicity, Charlie had agreed to participate.

Mike tried to visualize the manpower tied up with this investigation all over the country: hundreds of officers expending thousands of hours chasing one man whose imagination and sheer audacity had so far left everyone standing.

Reaching the path, Mike looked back down into the gully where Julia Norman had died.

Mike remembered Essie, her small body in his arms and plump little arms around his neck. He stood on the path, staring back at nothing, and wept.

This time Alastair Bowen had made a big effort to get through to Max. He'd sat opposite the other man, his hands idly playing with the cuttings books that lay on the table, and he'd begun to talk.

At first, Max had made a big show of not listening, but slowly Mike had seen him drawn into Alastair's tale. It seemed to Mike that Jake's father had gone to great lengths to dredge from his memory one of the few stories he could remember about Jake that had pleasure in it. And there had been a part for Max.

'I can remember,' Alastair said, 'the winter fair when you and Jake were both about seven years old. Jake was just coming up for eight in the New Year, but you were that little bit younger, weren't you, Max? A spring baby, where Jake was a winter child. I always thought that the winter fair marked the start of Christmas. Still almost a month to go, but there would be the smell of chestnuts in the air and the chill of that cold northerly that always seemed to blow across the valley. You both loved the fair, you and Jake. The noise and lights and all the fuss of unloading. You'd be out there, the pair of you, from the moment the first lorries arrived, getting in the way and hoping for a free ride when the men were setting up. You always reckoned you were going to run away one time when the fair came. One day, you'd say, the winter fair would leave town and take you with it.'

'I did one time,' Max said.

Alastair switched his gaze, focusing on Max. 'I remember,' he said. 'Your mam was going frantic, blaming me, blaming Jake. It was three days till the police fetched you back.'

'Should have let me be,' Max said. 'I'd have been all right.'

Slowly Alastair nodded. 'I guess you would,' he said. 'You'd have been away from Jake.'

A look of anger crossed Max's face and for a moment it seemed as though the rapport slowly being built up would fall apart, but Alastair pressed on.

'We didn't have a lot to spend. You'd both saved what bit of pocket money you'd got, saved for weeks, and I'd given you both a bit extra, I remember, but it was the deciding what to spend it on that took the time. Round that fair we went a dozen times, just taking it all in, till you and Jake decided which rides and which side-shows you'd go on.' He shook his head, a smile curving the corners of his mouth and a softness in his eyes. 'I don't know why you took so long, though. It would always be the same thing, year after year, from the first time I took you and you were old enough for anything other than the baby rides.'

Max returned the smile, both men now locked into the memory. 'The waltzers first,' Max said. 'Then the big wheel and the shooting gallery.' He grinned at Alastair, 'That was because you were good at it and Jake always wanted to go one better.'

'It took him another five years even to come close,' Alastair said, and there was pride in his voice, 'but he never gave it up, even though I always told him it was fixed. That you had to compensate for bad set-up and sights that weren't aligned and all you stood to win anyway was some stupid soft toy.'

'Jake never gave up on anything he started,' Max said. 'He always won in the end.'

'The funny thing, though,' Alastair said slowly,

'whatever else happened, you always finished up with the same ride. Even when I'd have thought you'd grown too big.'

'The carousel.' Max laughed aloud. 'It was magic, that thing. When we were little kids we'd sit up there on those painted horses and pretend that we could ride away for ever. I don't think Jake ever stopped thinking like that. We always wanted to ride real horses, but you never had the money for lessons and neither did my mam.' He laughed briefly. 'Closest we got were the seaside ponies. Old nags that never did anything but walk up and down between the breakwaters. The carousel was better all round.'

From his corner of the visitors' room Mike watched these two men, engrossed in their shared memories, with a kind of fascination. He didn't know how much of this was truth or how much a deliberately rose-coloured fabrication, but it was encouraging to see the developing rapport. Was this the breakthrough they had hoped for? He was unprepared for Alastair's sudden change of tack.

'What happened to that other film, Max? The other one you made with Jake?'

Max stared at him. 'I don't know what you mean,' he said.

'Oh, yes, I think you do. The one with the girl from the carousel. The pretty little thing that helped her brother take the money.'

Max stood up and turned towards the door. He's pushed him too far, Mike thought. Fuck it, I thought we were getting somewhere.

Then, abruptly, Max sat down again. 'It was Jake's

first experiment,' he said. 'It wasn't easy getting more film, but Jake had a bit of a job by then and so did I, so we managed. Got this girl to meet us after she'd finished. It wasn't hard, she liked Jake – everyone liked Jake. She was, you know, flattered like, that Jake was that bit older. She must have been thirteen, fourteen at most, but she had great little tits and we weren't the first she'd gone with.'

'You made the film in Jake's bedroom,' Alastair said.

'Yeah. Lighting was a big problem, but we improvised. Jake used the darkroom at school and he borrowed a photoflood bulb. Over the weekend, no one noticed it was missing. That helped a lot, and we brought up every lamp you'd got in the house and a big flashlight he'd got from somewhere. It worked OK. We got the girl drunk on cheap cider. She wasn't used to the stuff and it didn't take that much. She did pretty much anything we wanted after that. I filmed Jake and he filmed me. Jake had all these magazines he used to pinch. I mean, they were nothing special, not like the stuff Jake produced later on, but, you know teenage boys – all hormones and no sense of responsibility. It was a laugh.'

'Not for the girl,' Alastair said with a cold gentleness that took Mike by surprise. Alastair's anger at what Max was saying was as palpable as his own. 'And I don't think many teenage boys, even after reading mucky books, would tie an underage girl to the bed and rape her repeatedly, just for a good laugh.'

Max stood up again, his face stony, closed down once more. This time he called for the guard, demanding to be taken away.

'Why didn't you tell me about that other film?' Mike demanded when he had gone. 'You saw it and you didn't report Jake then?'

Alastair shook his head. 'I never saw it,' he said. 'I guessed from the rumours that were flying around and the accusations that Sally Wilson made. But no one believed her, even though the evidence was all there. Sally and her sister, they were known for it all over town and no one gave a damn.'

'That was why Max got equal credit on the other film,' Mike said quietly.

Alastair nodded. 'Yes,' he said. 'I believe it was.'

Chapter Nineteen

Little of use had happened over the weekend after Alastair's meeting with Max. They had talked on the return journey, Mike driving Alastair back to where he was staying, but Alastair had added only one thing to Mike's small fund of knowledge. Mostly, he seemed to want to be alone with his thoughts and resented Mike's intrusion.

'You realize that we could charge you?' Mike asked him at one point. The rain had begun again, falling in heavy drops against the windscreen. Alastair stared at it, an expression of concentration on his face.

'You could,' he conceded. 'I would not oppose you if you did.'

'You've obstructed a police investigation,' Mike persisted. 'Kept back evidence that could have saved lives. Protected Jake when you knew he had committed murder.'

'When I *suspected* he might have done, Inspector. I knew nothing for certain. I still know nothing for certain.'

'You're playing games, Alastair. This isn't a question of semantics, it's about people dying. About a child that might still be alive. It's about why the hell you kept quiet.'

He braked sharply, not having seen the car in front

signal to pull out. His hand poised above the horn until he realized it had been his own fault.

'I suggest you concentrate on your driving, Inspector,' Alastair told him with his infuriating calm. 'And watch your speed. You don't want to be seen breaking the law.'

Mike seethed but said nothing. He eased back on the accelerator, back from the eighty-five he'd been doing – far too fast for the driving rain.

'Why *did* you protect him, Alastair? I can understand any parent wanting to think the best of their son, but you despised Jake. You had no illusions about him.'

'Despise him? No, it wasn't that. I . . . pitied him.'

'I don't buy that, Alastair. I don't buy that at all.'

There was silence while Mike thought it through. Nothing Alastair had said so far explained his protection of his son. The key seemed to be Alastair's decision to wait until his wife had died before coming forward.

'What were you protecting your wife from?' Mike asked suddenly. 'What was it Jake knew about you that you were afraid she might find out?'

It was a long time before Alastair gave any response.

'There were things,' he said. 'Just things I had done.'

Mike had spent the Monday morning reviewing his notes and sitting in on the briefing Peterson had been giving to those still on house-to-house or following up the previous year's holiday traffic. It seemed an impossible task. Mike was bitterly aware, as was every officer from the most inexperienced probationer up, that the sheer quantity of information they had gathered could be working against them. Their man might already have been questioned, made a statement, even come forward with information. He might be on a dozen lists and, until the information was cross-referenced, the significance not be seen. Computers helped, but the information still had to be put onto the system and that took time. Other serial killers had fallen through the gaps just because of this kind of confusion: the problem of referencing and cross-referencing; of collating and making sense.

And there would be the *Crimewatch* programme the following night, with all the extra statements and witnesses and people who were trying to be helpful. They needed the exposure and they needed the support the programme would generate, but Mike and everyone else on the team dreaded the extra paperwork.

At midday Mike left Honiton to see Charlie Morrow. The road was choked with holiday traffic and Jake, parked in a side road and reading the morning paper, had little worry about being seen. He'd changed his location three times that morning, checking that Mike's car was still parked but risking being away for upwards of fifteen minutes at a time.

In Jake's mind this was giving the policeman the illusion of a sporting chance.

He kept a good distance behind on roads that offered little opportunity for turning off or overtaking, driving with the windows wide open, enjoying the summer sun.

Jake followed right up to the gates of the nursing

home and watched Mike go inside. Then he passed on by.

'I'd got used to seeing my face in the mirror,' Charlie said, 'but to go public like that, it was another thing entirely.'

Mike put the newspaper down and sat back in the easy chair. 'Are you sure you can cope with this television thing?' he asked. 'It's even more public than the newspapers. No one would blame you if you couldn't.'

'Wouldn't they? Maybe not, Mike, but I'd blame myself. This is no time for pissing about. That bastard's out there and I want to play my part in catching him.' He hesitated, then asked, 'There's been nothing more, I suppose?'

'On Essie? No, nothing. I spoke to Maria a few times over the weekend and we're in close contact with everyone on the case in Norwich, but so far there's been no word. We're into the second week now.' He shrugged helplessly. 'They've interviewed everyone who was in the area over and over again. Jake must have been convincing to get Essie even to talk to him. There's an alleyway running at the back of the school. We guess he must have taken her out that way.'

'And no one noticed anything wrong?'

'Essie was seen standing by the gate talking to a man. She was still on school premises at the time and the woman swears she saw her turn away as though she was about to cross the playground towards the other entrance. She was busy with her own kids and noticed nothing more. We've a couple of other similar sightings, but . . . well, I've been with Maria once or twice to pick up Essie. Kids and parents everywhere. Cars double-parked. It's pure chaos. It's not as hard to imagine as you might think. If Jake looked confident, and we know he would, then he might well go unnoticed.'

'And the man Essie was talking to?'

'Tall, sandy-haired, clean-shaven. Wearing jeans and a light-coloured shirt. Possibly blue, but that's about all we have. Another witness is convinced she saw the man bending down to tie Essie's shoe. She was wearing these little canvas lace-up things. She's still not that good at bows . . .' He trailed off, distracted, finding it hard to think that clearly about the little girl.

'Is Maria still with her sister?'

'No, she's gone back to Oaklands, Jo and her mother are staying with relatives. It seemed best to get her away from the media fuss.'

Charlie nodded. 'This *Crimewatch* thing, the whole programme's devoted to Jake Bowen, or so they tell me.'

'That's right. God knows, there's more than enough to fill it.'

'I'm sure he'll be well flattered,' Charlie said.

It was late afternoon by the time Mike got back to Honiton. He found Peterson and Alastair with others in the briefing room, making final reviews of the footage to be shown on *Crimewatch* the following day. Much of it could have been library film from any big case, showing officers on house-to-house, others in slow-moving lines, searching the fields around Colwell Barton.

He got water from the cooler and sat down, watching the screen. Peterson came over.

'That stuff's come in from up north,' he said. 'It's on your desk.'

'Anything useful?'

Peterson shrugged. 'All a bit vague. There's the counsellor's statement and a social worker's assessment based on a home visit. Plus Alastair's and Jake's statements to the police and another from his mother. Not a hell of a lot more. Alastair called the local vicar in as a character witness, that sort of thing.'

'You've shown Alastair?'

'Not yet. Thought I'd give you the pleasure. At least he talks to you.'

Mike smiled wryly. 'And you're telling me that's a good thing?' He sipped some water and tried to relax in the uncomfortable plastic chair. 'I still think we should charge him.' he said. 'Stop treating him with kid gloves and see what facing an obstruction charge would do for his recall.'

'I'm tempted to agree, Mike, but so far I've been vetoed. We're to see what we can get out of him this way, see what he can pull out of Max too. I mean, having Max in custody hasn't got a whole lot further and, frankly, I don't think Alastair gives a damn about it either way. It strikes me that, now his wife's gone, nothing matters to him very much.'

Mike shrugged. 'I don't know,' he admitted. 'It's funny, you'd think he'd want to talk about his wife, dying so recently. But he seems to have put her right out of his mind. Never mentions her unless I do.'

'I think he sees that as a personal matter,' Peterson suggested. 'Not something he would appreciate us trampling over.'

Mike thought about it, wondering again what Alastair had been keeping from his wife. Did she have her suspicions about Jake too? Or, as Alastair had insisted, did she continue to view Jake as a precious and innocent son?

'Charlie's all set for tomorrow,' he said. 'I thought maybe he'd have second thoughts, but he's going ahead with it.'

'That's good. I suggest we break early tonight, Mike. Sleep's been in short supply lately and we'll get none tomorrow night.'

'I won't argue,' Mike said. 'Look, I'll arrange for Alastair to be taken home, then try and get something to eat. I don't remember having lunch. Are your family holding up OK?'

Peterson nodded. 'As well as any of us are,' he said.

Jake had been waiting, parked in the side road he had used earlier. He'd been prepared to give them fifteen minutes more, then finish for the night. If they came out after that, well, then it was the luck of the game and a score for them.

He'd changed cars, swapping the red Sierra for a small green hatchback that he kept in a lock-up garage ready for occasional use, one of several he had scattered up and down the country.

Suddenly Peterson, Mike Croft and Alastair Bowen came out together and stood for a moment talking in the bright evening sunshine. Jake watched, seeing his father up close for the first time in almost eighteen years.

Mike left, alone, a few minutes later and it was a young officer in uniform who opened his car door for Alastair to get inside.

Jake watched them pull away, then waited for a slow count of ten before following, the anonymous little hatchback tailing a couple of cars behind on the Dorchester road.

Chapter Twenty

The house was at the end of a narrow lane, single-track with banks on either side, topped by an unclipped hedge. Jake had driven about a quarter of a mile past the entrance to the lane and parked the car on the verge at the side of the road, then walked back to find the best way of approaching the house unseen. By skirting back towards the main road, he found a gate and climbed over it into a field, then followed the hedge back the way he had come towards the house. It took over an hour and several detours – finding gaps in hedges, having to cut back into neighbouring fields, before Jake finally had the house in sight.

It was not the best of positions. He was quite exposed, crouched beside the hedge and at the top of the slight rise, and visibility was restricted. Jake could see only one side of the house and the path immediately in front of the door.

The house had a small garden in front and a larger one behind. A low fence separated it from the field. It was run down and overgrown, the once cultivated shrubs and brambles promising to provide much better cover when it finally grew dark.

The evening was warm and Jake lay in the sun barely moving, watching the house. Once a man who was not his father came out into the garden and walked down the path, casually glancing around. Once a face appeared at an upstairs window. But that was all.

At eight o'clock, Jake turned over on his back and closed his eyes. There was still sufficient heat in the sun and in the baked earth to satisfy him. Stretching out like a basking cat, he slept.

He woke after dark. Lights had gone on in the house and his watch told him that it was five past twelve. He could still see with little difficulty, his eyes accustomed to the summer dark that was still merely a velvet blue at this time of night and helped by a thin moon. Keeping to the shadows, Jake began to move towards the house. His trousers were a light grey and his shirt was pale. Anyone glancing from the house would probably have seen him despite his caution, but Jake paid no heed to that. It was a chance he'd have to take for now.

He got close enough to see through the unblinded windows and into the living room. His father and a second man sat watching the television. A single table-lamp was lit close to Alastair's chair. As Jake watched, the first man, the one he'd seen in the garden, came through the door with tea things on a tray. Jake ducked down as he came to pull the curtains closed, then moved around to the other side of the house.

The kitchen was in darkness, but the windows had neither curtains nor blinds and Jake could see inside. He moved to the back door, tried it. It was locked, but a cautious push at top and bottom moved it slightly against the frame. Not bolted then, just the single fastening. He completed his circuit of the house and stood for a brief time in the shadows beside the front door, listening to the night-time silence. Any noise he made forcing the back door would sound like a rifle crack in the still air.

Jake took the more direct route back to his car, following the narrow track to the road. Once there he put on the light summer jacket he'd had lying on the back seat. He kept a basic toolkit in his car. He took out a penknife and the wrench from his socket set, together with a flat-blade screwdriver and a roll of ducting tape. The screwdriver was nowhere near as long as he would have liked, but it would have to do. Then he made his way back towards the house, moving cautiously but quickly along the track.

Two lights burned in the house, one in an upstairs room and one in the living room that Jake had peered into earlier. Jake went around to the rear of the house and tried the back door again. Still locked but not bolted. He pushed against it, seeing how far he could ease it from the frame, and tried the screwdriver, forcing it into the gap. It was an easy fit.

He circled the house again, looking for open windows. The night was still warm and surely no one would be sleeping with them closed.

On the ground floor there was nothing, but upstairs the windows in the lighted room were open wide and the small window that probably led onto the landing was a little ajar. There was still the problem of getting up there, though.

Jake stepped back into deeper shadow and studied the situation. There was nothing to climb and his previous reconnaissance had shown no outbuildings that could hold a ladder.

Slowly, he retraced his steps. His watch told him that it was one fifteen, and the blue of evening had given way to a deeper night. He slid the screwdriver blade into the crack in the door and levered hard, trying to compensate for the shortness of the blade. He needn't have been concerned. The door gave easily with a loud crack as the wood splintered from the frame.

Jake stepped back into the deeper shade at the side of the part-open door, keeping his gaze focused on the ground so as not to be blinded as the light in the kitchen suddenly snapped on and poured through the window. The first man into the room saw the broken door. Jake heard him shout something to his colleague. Heard the footsteps on lino and then the door was wrenched wide. Jake's arm came down as the man ran outside. The blow landed badly, the wrench catching the man's shoulder on the downward stroke, enough to make him stumble but then begin to turn. But Jake's backhand caught his chin as he swung around and the man went down, his half-cry not loud, but echoing in the silence. Jake hit him again just to be sure and then again, even though he lay still. He could see the blood darkening the metal of the wrench and feel its slickness on his hand. Jake paused, to wipe his blood-marked palm on the other man's clothes, then moved on into the house.

The second officer had run upstairs to Alastair. He came down again, calling to his colleague as Jake stepped into the hall. The officer was trying to be calm, advancing slowly down the stairs, his hands a little outstretched and his voice as steady as he could make it, telling Jake to put his weapon down.

Jake took a step back towards the kitchen door, keeping his exit clear, and the officer seemed to take this move as uncertainty. But Jake was only repositioning for attack. This man was older, more experienced than the one he'd dealt with outside. Jake let the man come on, to give him the feeling that he might be getting somewhere, bring him close enough to strike and wait to see what opportunity offered him.

He lowered the wrench slightly, let his shoulders relax and took another step towards the door, the move bringing him around so he faced the bottom of the stairs. The officer took another step down, still talking to Jake, the tone calm and measured, more and more certain that he was in control.

Even when Alastair appeared on the landing, the man neither faltered nor turned, just raised his voice a little to tell Alastair not to move, then turned his attention back to Jake.

Jake allowed him one more step, then moved forward with a speed that had the man reeling even before the blow was struck. He fell forward, almost taking Jake with him, one hand clutching at what was left of the right eye, where Jake's blow had landed.

Jake did not wait to see what damage he had done. Alastair had taken a moment to respond, but now he was running. Jake took the stairs two at a time, catching up with him at the bedroom door, reaching forward to slam it just as his father's hand touched the handle.

'I think you should come with me,' Jake said.

*

Below him, in the hall, Jake could hear the policeman's voice. He must have a radio or a mobile. He obviously hadn't hit him hard enough.

He reached out and grabbed Alastair by the arm, swinging him around and twisting the wrist against the older man's back. Alastair gasped with pain, his knees buckling as his arm was taken further up his back. Jake kicked at Alastair's legs, dropping the wrench and grabbing at the other arm, pulling back so that his father hit the floor face-first. He bound Alastair's hands tightly with the ducting tape, opened the knife and picked up the wrench, which he shoved through the belt of his trousers. Then he pulled up on Alastair's bound hands and forced him to his feet, turning him around so that he could see the knife. Then, the knife blade pressed against Alastair's back, Jake forced him down the stairs. The officer he had injured still lay on the floor, blood pouring from his face, the eye closed and the surrounding skin already turning blue. Jake kicked the radio from the man's hand, then kicked the officer in the head, the blood spurting from the growing wound. He left him screaming on the hall floor as he forced Alastair out through the kitchen door and into the night.

Chapter Twenty-One

Mike was woken at two p.m. with the news that Alastair had gone and two officers were down. He was dressed and at the house only twenty minutes later.

First reports were confused. One officer, though wounded, had managed to call in. He didn't yet know about the other one. Road-blocks were being set up – Mike encountered one, hastily arranged, a police car pulled up across the road and an officer with a torch stopping what traffic there was – but they had little hope of tracking Jake. Fast as the response had been, he still had the jump on them.

An ambulance and two police cars, blue beacons creating artificial daylight, stood in front of the house. Peterson was on his way, Mike was told. One officer was still conscious, about to be taken away in the ambulance. The other had not been so lucky and had been declared dead at the scene.

'What happened here?' Mike asked one of the uniformed officers who'd been first on the scene.

'A bloody fuck-up,' the man said. 'We don't know for sure. Jenkins, the man who died, he was coming out of the back door when he was attacked. Bowen must have hit him about a half dozen times. Moran, he's likely to lose an eye, but he's lucky to be alive. And he's still conscious, sir, just. Claims he got a good look at our man.'

Mike glanced towards the ambulance. It was about to depart and he had no wish to delay it. 'You've someone going with him?'

'Yes, sir, and there's an ARV unit been actioned. If Bowen knows there's a witness, he might have a second go.'

Mike nodded, wondering what the hospital would make of an armed response unit in its emergency room. He was surprised that the man had been allowed to live. Did Jake think he was more seriously injured than he was, or had he been in too much of a hurry to finish the job?

He walked round to the back of the house. The body still lay on the floor, waiting for the duty surgeon and the pathologist to arrive. Some officers stood beside the fallen man, while others were still putting up a cordon, separating the house and gardens from the fields beyond. Light from the kitchen showed the way the lock had been forced, giving Jake access to those inside. It was, as the uniformed man had said, an almighty cock-up, Mike thought.

Peterson had arrived by the time Mike returned to the front of the house. He was talking to the uniformed police.

His face was grave as he came over to Mike. 'We're going to look even bigger bloody fools,' he said. 'And we've a dead officer into the bargain.'

'They should have been armed,' Mike said. 'It was madness to think Jake would pass this one by. I want protection for Charlie at least until the *Crimewatch* thing is over. And for Maria too, now she's no longer with her sister.'

Peterson nodded. 'Lot of good it did here,' he said.

Chapter Twenty-Two

Mike did not want Maria to hear about Alastair on the morning news, so he called her himself when he returned to Honiton at seven that morning. She was shocked, devastated. Mike had not realized that, emotionally, she had so much riding on being able to talk to Alastair Bowen; so much hope that he might lead them to Essie.

'I'm coming down to you,' Maria told him abruptly. 'I can't stand it, just sitting here, trying to work when there's nothing I can do to help.'

'Stay there, Maria. It's too dangerous here, you must see that.'

'Nowhere's safe, Mike, and no one, not until he's put away. Wherever I am he could come for me.'

'We'll arrange protection for you.'

'And much good that will do. Look, Mike, I won't be argued with.'

She hung up then and when Mike tried to call her back she'd switched to the answerphone.

Sighing, he put the receiver down, not bothering to leave a message she'd refuse to hear.

'Why don't you put an ad in some of the nationals?' Liz asked Charlie, 'or in the *Dorchester Herald*. We know he reads that. He knew all about Macey.'

They'd been listening to Charlie telling them about the message he'd left on the news groups. So far, there'd been no response from Jake Bowen.

'It's an idea,' Charlie agreed, 'though there's no guarantee he reads the small ads.'

Macey nodded thoughtfully. He'd come here to get Charlie's reaction to Alastair's kidnapping and to talk about the *Crimewatch* programme. Charlie's responses would make it into the late edition.

'How about the Lonely Hearts column?' Liz asked.

'Maybe,' Charlie agreed thoughtfully. Jake had been known to pick up potential models that way. 'I could give it a go, what is there to lose?'

Macey laughed harshly. 'Mark my words, advert or no advert, all you have to do is wait for long enough and Jakey boy will come to you.'

Liz ignored Macey's almost gleeful attitude. 'It should go in as a small display ad,' she said. 'We do them in bold type surrounded by little black hearts or flowers. Really makes them stand out.'

'Did it work for you, then?' Macey asked her. 'Or are you still looking, darling?'

Liz paid him no attention. 'What do you think?' she asked Charlie.

'That it's a good idea.' He pulled a pad and paper towards him. 'How many words can I have?'

'Best keep it short. I think you can have up to thirty words, but make it snappy.'

Charlie was deep in thought, doodling on the corner of the pad. 'It's got to be something he would know at once,' he said. 'What do people usually put in these things?'

'Oh, things in common, the sort of person you're looking for, that kind of thing.'

Charlie thought about it. 'Vincenza's place,' he said. Referring to the house where Jake had stored some of his more spectacular work. It was where Charlie had received his injuries, Jake having booby-trapped the safe he'd used for storage.

This was something Jake could hardly miss.

Charlie scribbled a sentence on the paper, amended it, scribbled again, then read out the result.

'J,' he said. 'Remember Vincent's place? We should meet again. Regards, Charlie.'

Jake watched his father wander through the basement rooms. He'd left the doors wide open and the camera running so that he could observe the old man passing from room to room on the CCTV screens, study his reaction to the different settings Jake used as backdrops for some of his more unusual films.

Alastair sat down briefly on the single bed in a room full of bondage equipment and decorated by a full-length mirror that covered most of one wall. Jake saw him studying himself in the mirror, a look of pain in his eyes and confusion, as though he wondered how he had found himself in such a place.

Then his father went back into the largest of the basement rooms. Essie lay on her pile of towels in one corner, sleeping restlessly. She'd had a fever this last day or two and Jake knew, as he watched his father go to her and touch her face with his fingertips, how dry and hot the skin would feel. He could sense it as though he felt it with his own hands.

She was quite seriously unwell. No real food, probably not enough fluids and the effects of such long periods of sedation had taken their toll.

Jake left his room with its bank of television screens and, with a sawn-off shotgun resting easily across his arm, went down to the basement, checking his father's position through a peephole in the door before going through.

'She's sick,' Alastair said as Jake entered.

'I know.'

'Why take the child, Jake? What do you plan to do with her?'

Jake sat down on the basement steps and pondered the question as though he'd given it no previous thought. 'I've not decided yet,' he said. 'I thought I'd leave that up to you.'

Alastair winced. 'What have I to do with it? I don't even know this child.'

'You need to know a child to care for her?' Jake asked. He sounded surprised. 'What do you think to my workplace, Alastair?'

'Your workplace. This is where you make that filth.'

'Some of it. The rest I make on location.' Jake smiled. 'Some real stars have lived here for a time. Julia Norman, for instance. Beautiful girl, and so versatile.'

'And does anyone survive this place?' Alastair asked

him. He was looking at the child, but, Jake guessed, thinking of himself.

'Not so far,' Jake admitted.

'And you plan to kill me too?'

Jake nodded slowly. 'I expect so,' he said. 'But not today. At least, not so long as you behave. They're doing a real Jake Bowen *This is Your Life* show on the television later on tonight, I thought you might like to watch it with me.'

Alastair shuddered, suddenly cold. 'And the child?' he asked again.

'Oh, she can watch too,' Jake said.

Chapter Twenty-Three

Late Tuesday evening Jake brought Alastair upstairs. He kept him covered with the shotgun and guided him into the living room, where the television was already on.

'Sit there,' he told him, directing Alastair to an old-fashioned dining carver, with wooden arms and a high back. He kept the gun pressed against Alastair's throat while he secured his hands to the chair with plastic cable-ties and his ankles to the front legs with tape. 'Behave yourself,' Jake told him, 'and I'll free one hand later, let you have a beer while we watch the programme.'

Alastair struggled against his bonds when Jake left the room, but it was of little use. The heavy plastic of the ties bit into his wrists and his efforts to move threatened only to overturn the chair. When Jake returned only moments later with Essie in his arms, Alastair had already given up. In his mind he had begun to prepare himself to die and he was amazed at how little it mattered any more.

Jake had put fresh towels on the sofa and he lay Essie down, propping her head with cushions. He'd given her no more of the sedative since midday and she was semi-conscious, restless and confused. She had started crying for her mother in the brief moments of lucidity that came and went, and watching them both on camera, Jake knew that her whimpering had begun to irritate Alastair.

'Quite a little family,' Jake commented, glancing at his father. He leaned over the child and whispered to her with a show of tenderness and deep concern, 'Be quiet, Essie baby. The film about your Uncle Jake's about to start and Uncle Mike might well be in it too.' He straightened up and turned back to his father. 'Now, about that beer.'

True to his word, he freed one of Alastair's hands, opened a can for him and let him hold it. He'd made popcorn too. Alastair watched as he gave a small piece to Essie, placing it in her mouth, but she couldn't chew, didn't even seem to realize that it was there. He shook his head as Jake waved the bowl in his direction, a chill running through him at the sight of his son's slight smile.

'Well, all the more for me then,' Jake said.

They sat together in the comfortable room, the large blue sofa piled high with cushions, the lights softly shaded and the curtains closed against the threat of a summer storm announced by a rising wind. Jake smiled and relaxed as his life story unfolded on the flickering screen. Alastair watched his son, unable to take his eyes from Jake's calm face.

On screen, the presenter said, 'We pick up the story of Jake Bowen when he was just fifteen years old and well known in his local community for a film of quite another kind.'

Jake had talked about himself as the next John Pilger, Alastair remembered, told local journalists that he had high hopes of a career as a documentary film-maker, righting wrongs and telling the world the truth. He'd been convincing too, almost persuaded Alastair on occasions.

'Ah, that was a great year,' Jake commented. 'You know the funny thing? I thought for a brief time that was where I wanted to be. Front line, changing the world.'

'Was that why you made the other film? Raped that girl?'

Jake raised an eyebrow. 'Oh, so you *do* know about that. I was never sure. Max tell you, did he?'

Alastair said nothing.

'It was the power thing,' Jake volunteered. 'That was it with both those films. A power thing. Pretty heady stuff when you're just fifteen, not that you'd understand that.'

'Understand what? I understand that you abused the trust we all put in you. Abused that girl too, you and Max.'

'What trust?' Jake asked mildly. 'Now, be quiet, I want to hear what they have to say.'

They sat in silence as Jake drank his beer and watched the TV; the slow procession of his life. Alastair in turn watched his son. They made little mention of the early films, the ones that built his reputation in the industry. Jake had still been living with his parents then, and Alastair remembered the shock he had felt when he had realized what kind of films his son made. Jake had been proud of what he did, though, talked about it like an art form, always pushing the envelope of acceptability, always fighting for the best production values he could get with the equipment he could afford. Alastair knew it would annoy his son, though he gave no outward sign, when the presenter merely skipped through a brief commentary of Jake's early career in film, noting only that he first came to police attention after a raid on a sex shop in a Leeds back street. They missed out too on what Jake had described as his constant search for authenticity, mentioning only that he sometimes intercut his images with library footage and seemed to have an obsession with the links between sex and death.

Charlie Morrow described the day he had been injured in the blast that Bowen had prepared, his burns showing in every detail in the studio lights, every ridge and furrow that mapped his face, the way the dead skin pulled at the corner of his mouth and half closed one eye. Alastair watched as Jake leaned forward to get a closer look.

'Wonderful,' Jake whispered softly to himself. 'A wonderful effect.' He glanced across at Alastair. 'Do you know,' he asked him, 'just how much it would cost to produce something like that? You'd need a top effects artist to get it any other way.'

Alastair had no reply.

They moved on then to Jake's more recent crimes. The killing of a woman called Marion O'Donnel, whose body was found in a burning car. The murders of Caldwell and the others and finally the death of Julia Norman only two weeks before.

Jake sat forward, watching intently as Peterson talked about the latest outrage.

'This young woman was a gifted artist with a stunning future ahead of her. The death of a young person is always tragic, but this, this needless, wasteful death, seems to me especially sad. As if this is not difficult enough to deal with, we have reason to believe that Jake Bowen is implicated in the kidnapping of a young child, Essie Holmes, snatched from outside her school.'

'You take a good picture,' Jake remarked to the child as an image of Essie dressed in her school clothes filled the screen. He listened with the most rapt attention as they talked of witness statements and repeated the appeal made earlier by Essie's grandmother and Maria. They finished the account with an excerpt from the video of Julia, with Jake's voice enhanced and the sound cleaned up, giving instruction about how to move, how to pose, what to do to turn the punters on, and finishing with Jake's laughter as the girl told him some silly joke that even the enhanced tape couldn't catch.

Alastair heard the laughter and felt despair. 'Let the child go. She's no earthly use to you.'

Jake frowned. 'No imagination if you think that,' he said.

'The child will die, Jake. Let her go, or finish this whole thing now.'

Jake looked at his father in mild surprise. 'You'd like me to kill you both now?' he asked. 'Didn't think you were so ready for it, Alastair.'

The programme had reached the description of Alastair's abduction the night before. Jake laughed when he heard about the officer killed in the 'vicious attack', his laughter louder and less restrained at the mention of the bravery of the other officer, who, despite his wounds, had managed to call for help.

'We came very close to Jake Bowen last night,'

Peterson was saying, 'and we know he's getting over-confident, that he will get careless. We would appeal to him to give himself up. We accept that he probably needs help as much as he deserves blame, and he has nothing to fear in coming forward. Someone somewhere knows who Jake Bowen is and where he is. They must know that they're protecting a killer or at least suspect that something is amiss. Someone has suspicions – has doubts about a loved one or worries that a neighbour might not be all he seems.'

Jake was shouting quite uproariously now. 'Do you have doubts about a loved one, Father, or suspect I might be something not quite pleasant? Oh, come on, Alastair, you must see the joke.'

Alastair just stared at him. 'Why do this, Jake? Why cause all this suffering?'

Jake shook his head, bringing his laughter slowly under control.

'You don't get it, do you?' he said. 'You really don't.' He gestured with his beer in Essie's direction. 'You see it never was a question of *why*, Alastair. It was just a question of, well, *why not*?'

Chapter Twenty-Four

Wednesday morning at five o'clock Mike arrived back at Honiton. They had been manning the phones for most of the night, taking calls, finally closing the lines at three in the morning.

Driving back on empty roads, watching the sun come up, Mike was filled with a sense of unreality. The TV studio and Jake Bowen seemed to belong to another world. He wanted nothing more than to grab a few hours' sleep and forget everything for a while.

He was surprised to see Maria's car parked outside the pub where he was staying. He'd tried several times the day before to speak to her again, only getting the answerphone. When she hadn't appeared that afternoon or early evening, he had assumed that she had changed her mind and was just giving them both time to cool down.

Maria was asleep in the front of the car, the seat reclining as far as it would go and an old travel rug thrown over her legs. He tapped gently on the window. She woke and smiled, then opened the door and slipped into his arms.

Mike forgot he was supposed to be angry. 'God, I've missed you,' he said. 'When did you arrive?'

'Late last night. Well, early this morning really. The hotel was all shut up so I slept here.'

Mike had a pass key for the front door. He let them both in and took Maria up to his room.

'It's not a massive bed,' he told her.

She smiled. 'I'm sure we can manage. Anyway, I think we're both so tired we could sleep anywhere just now.'

'Sleep?' he questioned. 'I haven't seen you in so long.'

'If you're serious about that in half an hour, let me know. That's if you're still awake.'

He sat on the side of the bed and watched her undress, too tired even to remove his shoes. He finally shed his clothes and lay beside her, too much aware that he needed a shower and that he couldn't remember the last time he had shaved. Her body felt so wonderful curved against his own and the rhythm of her breathing so soothing as she drifted into sleep. Half an hour later, Mike was not awake to tell her anything at all.

Jake had locked both Alastair and Essie in one of the smaller rooms so that when he brought their breakfast down he could carry the tray without having to trouble with the gun.

He went to the top of the basement stairs to retrieve it before letting Alastair back into the outer room, locking the main door and slipping the key into his pocket.

Urging Alastair into the outer room at gunpoint, Jake returned to the smaller room to check on Essie, aware that his father still hovered near the door, watching him.

As Jake bent over the child, Alastair made his move. He had in his hands one of the leather straps taken from the bondage room and leapt at Jake as he knelt beside Essie's makeshift bed, the strap between his hands as though he planned to strangle Jake from behind.

Jake was ready for him, rising to his feet and striking backwards with the stock of the gun, hitting Alastair hard enough on the temple to send him, dazed and reeling, across the room.

'Just what did you plan to do?' he asked him. 'Strangle me? Do you even know how, Daddy dearest? And were you planning on taking the child with you? Or did you just think about your own skin? You'll have to try a damned sight harder than that, Alastair. A bloody sight harder.'

He left his father lying there and returned upstairs to watch them from his viewing room. Jake felt pleasantly surprised at his father's actions. He hadn't really thought the old man had it in him to try and fight.

Max Harriman had already heard the news about Alastair's kidnapping when Mike arrived to see him. Max was excited, unable to sit still. The one thing on his mind was how much they'd need him now the competition had been removed.

'He'll kill him, you know,' Max told Mike gleefully. 'Jake hates his father. Really, really loathes that man.'

'Why?' Mike asked him. 'What did Alastair do to make Jake hate him so much, and why wait all this time? He could have got rid of Alastair long ago.'

Max stopped his pacing and stood still, shaking his head. 'I told you, Jake hates his father. The way Alastair treated him all his life. He robbed him of his childhood, you know. Beat him, denied him all trace of affection. He was never a father to him. Never.'

'No, I don't buy that, Max. When I brought Alastair here you were talking about what must have been good times. When Alastair took you to the fair, those times you all shared together.' He leaned forward across the table. 'I need you, Max,' he said, sensing that flattery was going to get him further just now than any other means. 'Explain it to me, what went on between the pair of them that grew so much hate?'

Max hesitated for a moment, then sat down facing Mike.

'It isn't easy to explain,' he said. 'I mean, both parts of it were true. They were locked into this . . . this circle, like they were playing games with one another. One minute Alastair would be all over Jake, spoiling him, buying him new toys, taking him out. Then you'd look round and he'd have got mad with Jake about something and he'd be beating seven shades out of his backside. Or throwing all the stuff he'd bought him on the bonfire. Jake said to me once he had to learn fast not to cry out when his dad hit him. I could never understand that, because if he didn't yell, Alastair would hit him even harder. It'd been me, I'd have yelled the place down and begged for mercy on the first hit.'

'But Jake saw it as a challenge?'

'Must have done. He saw it as a kind of test, I suppose. Like, how much stronger than his dad could he be? It was like I said, they were locked into this kind of game. Jake never played with any of the stuff his dad bought. He said he never knew how long he'd have it, so what was the point? What his mam bought, though, that was different. One Christmas, we both had an Action Man. We used to take them up to the old allotments at the back of the school and have mock battles and stuff.'

'And Jake's mother bought that for him?'

Max nodded.

'And did Alastair never try to destroy those toys, the ones his mother had bought for him?'

Max laughed. 'You've got to be joking, Inspector Croft. The woman had forearms the size of hams and a left hook like you'd see from Mike Tyson. Alastair wouldn't dare to cross that woman.'

This was a new element. Was it true? Mike asked himself. 'And yet,' he said, 'she stood by and let her husband beat Jake? Beat him so badly that at one time it almost got to court?'

'Oh, you heard about that, did you? That was a laugh and a half.'

'I don't understand.'

Max sighed patiently. 'Jake thought it was a big joke,' he said. 'He was, what, thirteen, fourteen, and already he could have the average female doing back-flips. That woman, she would have done anything for Jake. It was such a joke, when he said he'd been stringing her along all the time. There was a right stink. He'd had the police involved and all sorts. Alastair ranting and demanding an apology, and this woman, her career was fucked up before she'd even begun.'

'But it was the truth, wasn't it, Max? Alastair was guilty of cruelty.'

Max shrugged. 'That's not the point, Inspector, he would never have seen his dad go down for it.'

'Why not?' Mike pressed him. 'What linked those two? They hated each other and yet Alastair constantly protected his son and Jake seems to have done the same. And I don't understand what Jake's mother did about it all. She allowed this to go on and yet I get the impression that Jake loved her and that Alastair did too. And you say that they were afraid of her?'

Max Harriman was silent for a while, as though thinking it over. 'They were scared of her,' he said at last. 'Alastair knew what Jake was, what he did. But she wouldn't have it.'

'But she backed the idea that Jake get counselling.'

'Why not? She blamed Alastair, she blamed the school, she blamed everyone bar Jake when she thought he was going off the rails, playing truant and that. I don't know what it was, Inspector Croft. Maybe, well, she'd lost two or three babies before Jake came along. It must have been hard to accept that your kid was a problem child.' Max grinned. 'There wasn't a thing that frightened Jake. Nothing he couldn't or wouldn't do, even from being a kid. He always said that the biggest kick you could get out of life was doing all the things that people were afraid of doing and watching their faces while you did them. That was power to Jake. He used to say that you had to teach yourself not to be afraid. That anyone could do it, it just meant challenging yourself a little bit more each time until one day you realized you weren't scared of anything any more. You could do whatever you wanted. He said people were always asking themselves "Why?" whenever stuff went wrong. Jake always said they should be asking themselves why not.'

'But you said that he was afraid of his mother.'

Max nodded. 'But not later on. I think he respected her, kind of. She was tough, you see, as tough as Jake. She kept that family going by working all hours, more than Alastair ever did. He was in work, then out of it again. He was a lay preacher at the local church and that was what really mattered in his life.'

'But he left that, suddenly, and went to live in York.'

Max shrugged. 'Caught with his hand in the collection plate, wasn't he?'

'Alastair?'

'Yes, Alastair. Oh, it wasn't the first time, but this time he couldn't cover it up. He had a drink problem, and every now and then he fell off the wagon. This was one time.'

Mike absorbed that slowly. 'And was that why he beat Jake, when he was drunk?'

'No, no. You take things so literally. Look, the only one Alastair hurt when he was blitzed was himself. He'd fall over things, run into things, whatever. Someone would find him in the street and take him home. Anyone got knocked about then, it was Alastair. She'd lay into him with whatever came handy.' Max laughed, the memory obviously amusing him.

Mike tried to take all of this on board. 'I still don't understand,' he said. 'Why did Jake's mother allow the physical abuse to go on?'

'She didn't know about a lot of it,' he said, shrugging. 'Anyway, she wasn't one to spare the rod and spoil the child herself. When Jake cheeked her she'd backhand him and not think twice.'

'But is that the same thing? What we're talking about with Alastair is a systematic pattern of abuse.'

Max sighed and stared down at his hands, laying them flat upon the table. 'Alastair thought he was doing right,' he said. 'Thought Jake had the devil in him, and maybe he was right. Jake could outfox the devil, if you ask me. And his mam, well, I don't know. Maybe she didn't know the half of it. Maybe she thought it was up to his dad to punish him. And she always knew how sorry he'd be afterwards. Alastair would always be so terribly sorry. He'd go out and work all the overtime he could, bring in more money than usual, spend time doing stuff around the house. I don't know, maybe it was just the way things were.'

Mike looked thoughtfully at Max, uncertain of how much he really understood about Jake's family and how much truth there was in what Max said. So much seemed contradictory. He wondered how much further he could push things that day.

'Did Jake kill your mother?' he asked.

Max blinked in surprise. 'He didn't need to,' he said cryptically, 'she was already dead. All Jake did was stop the breathing.'

Maria should probably not have been in the incident room, Peterson thought, but she was a difficult lady to keep out of anything, and anyway he had no inclination to try.

'We've got a team of forensic psychologists and behavioural experts working on this, but if you ask me they can't agree on a damn thing.'

Maria grinned. 'That's the problem with shrinks,' she said. 'Have you heard the light-bulb joke?'

Peterson shook his head.

'How many shrinks does it take to change a light bulb?'

'I couldn't tell you.'

'One to change the light bulb, at least two to counsel the light bulb on the experience of coming out and half a dozen students to write up the research papers.'

Peterson laughed. 'You missed out the pop psychologist to write the coffee-table book,' he said, 'and a couple of tabloids to plaster it all over the front page.'

'And someone to propose the conspiracy theory,' Maria added. 'You said I could see those pictures?'

Peterson had the file in his hand. He lay on the table the photographs that had been sent to his daughter.

'She's still in shock,' he said. 'Won't let the kids out of her sight, though I can't say I blame her. I don't mind admitting, Maria, this has about finished me with the force. I got shifted into this, so they said, because of my experience. Head the investigations, they said, and I've got to admit that at first it was good to be hands-on again. Superintendents are desk jockeys these days. Glorified bloody administrators, hassling the troops into getting an optimum clear-up rate or whatever the current jargon is. But I have to tell you, I'd as soon be back behind my desk again. I sometimes wonder if I'm losing it.'

Maria shook her head. 'You know you're not,' she said. 'You're just under incredible stress . . . we all are.'

Maria looked more closely at the images Peterson had spread upon the table, the young children playing in the garden, with the mocking injuries marked upon their bodies. She fought hard to hold on to her professional calm.

'He's subtle,' she said quietly. 'And he knows exactly how much all this is going to hurt.'

The phone on Peterson's desk began to ring. He picked up the receiver, listened for several minutes, then scribbled something on the notepad on his desk.

'That was Mike,' he said, looking excited, animated. 'Max came through with something, a London address. He claims that Jake rented a flat and uses it as a letter drop.'

Chapter Twenty-Five

It was a beautiful evening after a perfect summer day. Jake stood on the clifftop looking out to sea, watching a lone cormorant skimming the waves, its prehistoric shape black against the grey-blue waters.

Alastair stood a few feet away, his hands unbound, the short-barrelled shotgun Jake held cradled across his body enough to keep him from running.

'I love this place,' Jake told him. 'It took me nearly two years to find it and another two to restore, but it's been worth every penny.'

Alastair turned his head slightly to regard his son. 'It's pleasant enough,' he said, 'but I wouldn't like to be this close to the cliff edge. Another year or two and this whole thing could be washed away.'

'I doubt that,' Jake said. 'This place will see us both dead and gone.'

Alastair said nothing but followed Jake's gaze, looking far out to the horizon. It seemed such a barren, lonely vista. Would anyone hear him if he called out? Or was everything as empty as this damned view of open ocean?

'What are you going to do with me?' he asked.

'Talk to you, for a while anyway. There are things I want to know, Alastair. This seems like it could be a good time.'

'As good as any,' Alastair said slowly. 'What is it I can tell you?'

Jake glanced at him. 'Did you ever love me?' he asked.

'Love you? Of course I did, you were my son.'

'Is that an answer? I don't think so.'

'It's the only one I can give. I did my best for you, Jake. Gave you all I could.'

'You gave me all you could,' Jake repeated thoughtfully. 'And what was that, Alastair? You gave me your hatred and a taste of the belt at least once a week just in case I'd done something you didn't catch me at. You told me I was bad even when I tried to do my best to be good. You made your own story in your head and, by God, you lived by it, and I never understood why you hated me so much. What it was that I had done to you that forced you to write me off practically before I was born and never, ever revise that view whatever I said. Whatever I did. I want to know it, Alastair, what it was that made you feel that way?'

Alastair shifted restlessly under his son's relentless gaze. Jake's voice was calm, as though he'd asked about the weather or some odd item of the news. Alastair wanted to deny his words, to tell him that he'd misunderstood, but he could not bring himself to lie.

'Even when you were a little child,' he said, 'you had that way with you, of doing things or saying things that only caused us pain. You were always evil, Jake, killing and maiming and telling lies. Creating hurt and pain where there'd been none before. I had to hurt you, Jake, show you what the pain meant. That you couldn't go on with your vile games and your lies and your... your deceits.'

'Ah, but they weren't deceits, were they, father? Not all of them, not in the beginning, and I know where all of this began, Alastair. Thinking about it, I really do, and it's so simple that it's almost laughable. That day I caught you with that woman in my mother's room. You on top of her, pounding away, with your white arse showing and your trousers down around your ankles. You'd not even taken time to get undressed before you started poking her. And she was squealing like some stuck pig. That's when it all began between us, your resentment of me. And all your lies about me won't change any of that.'

'It wasn't like that,' Alastair began to protest. 'You were far too young to understand. After you were born, I never went near your mother again. She wouldn't have me even touch her, scared she'd get pregnant again and lose another one. Or maybe have another like you, I don't know.'

'You're right, I wasn't old enough to understand,' Jake said, 'but you decided I was old enough to take your belt to. I was beaten raw, and all the time you were lying and screaming what an evil little bastard I'd turned out to be, and I can remember the pain of it. And the worst pain of all was not knowing what I was being punished for.'

'I was desperate,' Alastair protested. 'I loved your mother and I knew she'd never forgive me.'

'Not again, you mean. Not after all the other women.'

'I know that I was wrong,' Alastair said slowly,

spacing out his words as though to give them weight. 'And I regret all that, Jake, I really do. But you were never easy . . .'

'And when she came home and the neighbours told her what you'd been about. The lies you told her, about me killing her blasted cat. And you hitting it with that broken line prop until you broke its bloody back. I watched you bury it, and I heard her crying because she thought I was turning out like you and couldn't bear the thought of that. And you know what, Alastair? I could still taste the blood in my mouth where I'd bitten my tongue when you'd knocked me down. You'd given me a real gift that day, you'd taught me that you were weak and stupid and helpless and that I didn't have to be like you.'

Alastair stared out towards the darkening horizon, his jaw clenched and his body tight and rigid.

'I didn't make you the way you are,' he said. 'Nothing I did or didn't do taught you to be what you became, Jake, and you know that. If I lied about the details, I didn't lie about the rest. You were evil as a child, even more evil as an adult, and you had more scope to play your games. I never had a part in that.'

'You created me,' Jake told him mildly. 'Sowed the seed in my mother's belly. I'm sad for you that you didn't like the results.'

He turned his face away from his father, gazing once more out to sea. 'No, but you're right, of course. You had nothing to do with what I became. You wouldn't have begun to know how to do that. You never had that much about you, anything like the skill or the imagination to create someone like me.' He paused reflectively. 'It's sad, don't you think, that a father should despise his son so much or a son so hate the father?'

'If you hated me so much,' Alastair questioned harshly, 'why didn't you finish me off? Get rid of me earlier?'

'Why should I waste my time? It was much more fun to know that you were waiting, every day of your life, you were waiting for me to come back and you were living your life in fear. I enjoyed that, Alastair. Enjoyed that so much.' He sighed, as though suddenly weary of the game. 'Move closer to the edge, Alastair, and then look down. Go on.'

Reluctantly, the older man moved forward.

When Jake spoke to him, his voice was soft. 'Have you ever thought what it would be like to go on walking? To look down at that rush of white water scouring away at the cliff and just become a part of it all. To let go and leave all of this behind. Look down. Spread your arms and fall into the wind. Ask yourself just what it is you have to lose, what you have left. It's all finished for you, Alastair, this life. Why not let it go?'

Jake had moved closer to him, picking up from the grass the palm-sized digital camera he had left lying there. He lifted it to his eye, gun in one hand and the camera in the other, watching his father's face.

'It would be so easy,' Jake told him gently. 'You could make your peace with the world and then just let it all go.'

Alastair stood at the very edge of the cliff, his eyes

fixed on the boiling rush of water foaming on the rocks, then he jerked around to face Jake.

'I won't do it!' he shouted at his son. 'If you want me dead, you'll have to be the one to kill me.'

Jake fired then, hitting Alastair with both barrels full in the face, then trained the camera on his father's body as it spiralled down, arms stretched upon the wind, the splash tiny as it hit the sea.

Chapter Twenty-Six

Honiton had become the focus for something of a media circus following the *Crimewatch* programme, although with the coming of evening things had quietened down a little, journalists and photographers wandering off to pick up some local colour in the pubs.

Mike, Peterson and Maria had driven a dozen miles to find a quiet place to eat. They'd found a little restaurant in Lyme Regis, the relative anonymity of the seaside town promising them the chance of a quieter evening.

The raid had taken place on Jake's London flat and they were still waiting for reports to come in. A quantity of letters and what appeared to be house agents' details had been found, some of them going back four or five years. Mike had arranged for everything to be faxed through to him in Honiton, together with the first of the witness statements from neighbours. It would take time to arrive and everyone needed a break, so Peterson had suggested they all go and eat.

It had not been an easy day, Maria thought. She'd stayed inside avoiding the media crush, wanting to be useful yet so much aware that she had no real business being there. She'd prowled around the incident room, making tea, washing mugs and emptying bins, anything to keep busy, until Peterson had taken pity on her and given her the psychological reports to read.

'The problem is,' she said, picking up on an earlier conversation, 'there's so much pressure now to get it right. The public expect that anyone with half a degree in any of the mind sciences can get inside the killer's head and anticipate exactly what he's going to do.'

'There've been some spectacular successes,' Mike argued. 'The Jamie Bulger case, for instance, and early stuff on that London rapist working the railway stations.'

'John Duffy,' Peterson provided. 'That was a first. Then the floodgates opened.'

'And the level of expectation sky-rocketed.'

Maria paused as the waitress arrived, aware of the look the woman gave her and wondering if she'd been recognized. She carried on.

'The problem is the notion that you can be right all the time, and with Jake Bowen that's not easy. The man is ordered and intelligent. He doesn't seem to act from fear or impulse, he plans. And my guess is he's read all the same books we have.'

'Would you class him as a psychopath?' Peterson asked her. 'There seems to be some debate even about that.'

Maria prodded at the food on her plate. She was hungry but found it hard to eat, guilty about even that simple act of normality. 'It's a more complex question than you might think,' she said. 'For what it's worth, I don't believe I would. Neither do I think Jake Bowen is insane. My guess, and that's all it is, is that Jake knows exactly what he's doing and exactly what effect it's going to have. That he's capable even of becoming emotionally involved with those he hurts and kills. I think Jake Bowen understands what we would call right and wrong, can even empathize with it. I just don't think he cares.' She lay her fork down and poured water with a hand that trembled only slightly. 'That's what scares me so much.'

Macey had been out all day and Charlie only reached him at his home number late that evening.

'There's been no joy,' Charlie said. 'No replies to the ad as yet. I've been sitting by the phone, staring at it like a lovesick teenager. Anything your end?'

'Little things here and there, nothing conclusive. Your friend Peterson's had road-blocks all over the place, disrupting the holiday traffic, and the national press and TV've been out in force. It's been all right from my point of view. They've all been so bloody bored, I've been the most interesting thing around today. If I'd taken up all the offers of drink I'd had I'd have been comatose by now.'

Charlie laughed. 'So it's the move to London next, is it?'

'Living in hope, Charlie. Look, how long do you want this ad to run? Some bright spark on the force is going to see it and then the shit's really going to hit the fan. Depends whether you're bothered about that, of course?'

'Give it another day,' Charlie said. 'If he makes contact we're going to have to bring Mike in on it anyway, but if it comes to nothing I'd as soon not have him, well . . . bothered. We'll cross that bridge if and when we have to.'

'I can just see the headline, Charlie, "Injured Cop and Maverick Reporter Snare Woodland Killer". You know, it's a funny thing, but no one's come up with a tag for this one. He's not the something ripper or the what's-it strangler or the wherever poisoner.'

'Problem is, Macey, there's too much variety in what he does and he's too mobile. You know how folk like to pigeon-hole. Jake's problem is he wants everything.'

'Yeah, right. But he ought to have a tag line.'

'If he phones I'll recommend he gets a publicist,' Charlie promised.

He put the phone down and stared at it, willing it to ring. For all his attempt at humour, Charlie was finding this harder and harder to cope with. He knew that everyone involved in the Bowen investigation must feel the same. It was the not knowing, the feeling that Jake could be anywhere, that made it so hard to be rational. Charlie Morrow was no coward, but he wondered what he was going to do if Jake really did make that call.

When they arrived back at Honiton a pile of faxes awaited them. Half a dozen officers sat at their desks, working the late shift, still sifting through the phone calls that had come in the night before. *Crimewatch* had generated over 700 calls and a list of 270 names. Most would turn out to be entirely innocent; a few would be vindictive. Three or four names had come up more than once, and that might or might not be promising. All needed feeding into the database and cross-referencing with what information they'd already got.

Maria had gone in with them, her presence accepted but not mentioned. She had the feeling that as long as she kept her mouth shut, so would everyone else, and when Mike picked up a stack of papers from the newly faxed pile, so did she.

'What am I looking for?' she said.

Peterson raised an eyebrow. 'Try and establish some kind of order,' he said at last. 'Sort the documents by type and then by date. Then we'll list them, see if we can establish a pattern and if it fits with what else we've got.'

Mike was reading another fax.

'They talked to the cleaning lady,' he said. 'They got lucky, she lives only a few doors away. It's one of those converted houses,' he explained, 'and the other tenants knew who she was.'

'Was she helpful?' Peterson asked.

'Well, it sheds some light in one way but complicates it in others. She met the tenant only once, but apparently there are a number of people who stay there on an irregular basis. She thinks they're actors of some kind, which fits with what we know, but she said she didn't ask too many questions.'

'How does she get paid?' Maria asked.

'By post, once a month, in cash. It arrives on the twenty-eighth of every month in a padded envelope. When there are people staying there, she doesn't have to clean, but she gets paid the same anyway. If she has to do extra cleaning when they've gone, she gets paid an extra three hours, so obviously Jake must know who's in residence and approximately when.'

'It also means that quite a few people have keys, presumably.'

'Apparently.' Mike referred back to the fax. 'There are regulars who don't stay there but just pick up their mail. She's got instructions to leave the mail on the table in the hall until the Sunday. Any uncollected mail gets put in the sideboard cupboard in the living room. She thinks someone goes through it from time to time, and presumably those using it as a mail drop know where to look for stray letters.'

'The rest just gets left there,' Peterson commented, looking at the pile of faxes on the table. 'How long has she been doing the cleaning?'

Mike scanned the fax again. 'Three years, I think. Yes, that's right. She was recommended by the previous woman, a Mrs Lee, who's moved to Bangor apparently. They were neighbours. That was the only time she met the real tenant. The flat's rented under the name of Matthews. They're trying to find the landlord now, see how Jake pays his rent.'

'My guess is cash in a padded envelope,' Maria said. 'I don't suppose the landlord cares as long as Jake pays his rent and doesn't wreck the place.'

'They must have a way of contacting Bowen,' Peterson said. 'I mean, when the cleaning lady left, how did she let him know?'

Mike put the fax back on the table and sat down. 'He calls once a month,' he said. 'Her home address, since there's no direct line to the flat, only a communal phone in the hall. Just checks that she's got the money, asks if anything's needed and that's it. Apparently he asked this Mrs Lee if she knew of anyone who could help and gave her a bonus for finding someone.'

'And no one got curious or suspicious, because they were well paid and not being asked to do anything illegal,' Peterson concluded. 'Do we know when Jake's due to phone her again?'

'Last Tuesday,' Mike told him. 'We're a month adrift on that one. They're keeping a twenty-four-hour surveillance on the flat for the next few days, but the raid was hardly unobtrusive. I'd guess the most we can hope for is one of the regulars picking up their mail.'

'Could lead us somewhere. It's the best we've got so far.'

Maria was sorting through the lists of house agents' notes. Some were two or three pages long and had become separated during faxing, so she began putting them in order and stapling them back together, the simple task soothing, taking just enough of her concentration.

'He's looking for a place to restore, by the looks of these,' she said. 'Or at least, he was five years ago.'

Peterson pulled the small stack of collated sheets towards him and skimmed through. 'Older properties, detached, and with large gardens.'

'Hmm, and all of them with outbuildings or basements or both,' Maria added. 'Only one problem.'

'What's that?'

'If these are the ones Jake left in London, then they're obviously the ones he didn't want.'

Chapter Twenty-Seven

Thursday morning emerged out of a light drizzle that looked like nothing and soaked everything it touched. Jake had decided it was time to go back to work. The new samples he had ordered had come in and he was eager for a change of scene.

He felt an enormous sense of relief now that Alastair had left him. It was something he had waited a long time for and now that it had happened the euphoria was such that Jake wanted to share it.

The pity was that he had no one to tell. That was the good thing about film, knowing that it could be shared, that somewhere along the line there would be feedback from delighted fans.

The film of Alastair's demise was not enough on its own, but sooner or later Jake knew he'd find a way to work it into something special.

He liked driving in the rain. He enjoyed the sense of isolation, of separateness, being in the shelter of his car and watching the world around him disintegrate into millions upon millions of fragmented pieces. He liked the way the windscreen wipers, sweeping across the screen, restored his world for a merest instant before the rain shattered it once more. Deliberately, he set the wipers on single stroke rather than repeat, to make the most of the effect. It was a very visual, very Jake Bowen thing.

There was still the problem of what to do with Essie. Now Alastair had gone, he'd increased the sedation, hoping the dose was right, so she'd be certain not to wake before his return. The truth was, Jake had no real interest in the child.

He could film Essie – dead or alive or dying, she had financial potential – but was that what he really wanted to do? He guessed that everyone had written her off for dead by now; that they were hunting for a corpse and not a living child. Jake wondered if it would be more fun to let them know that Essie was still alive and then stand back and watch the response.

Whatever, he thought, he would have to take action soon, the child was definitely sick and he wasn't sure how much longer she would last.

Jake could not have anticipated Alastair's body being found so soon, but he had taken no account of the strong current that whipped around the headland and struck the foot of the cliffs, only to be turned back out to sea. The body, its shattered face battered by the ocean currents, fetched up on a stony beach only miles from where it had entered the water. Mike was sent to identify it.

'It isn't pretty,' the pathologist told him. 'I'll try and fit the post-mortem in some time today, but I can't promise anything.'

'Cause of death was gunshot wounds?' Mike asked.

'To that, a provisional yes,' the pathologist told him. 'Unless the shotgun was used to hide something else, of course. But whether or not he was dead at the precise moment he hit the water, well, I think that's pretty academic, don't you, considering half his face was blown away?'

Mike didn't feel qualified to comment. He had a sudden vision of Jake Bowen standing in a courtroom arguing it out with the prosecution, but he let it be.

'We've had dental records sent for,' he said. 'Will they be of any use?'

'Oh, yes. There are still plenty of teeth left. Most of the injury is to the upper portion of the head.'

They entered the small room at the side of the mortuary that was usually set aside for relatives identifying their dead.

'I put him in here,' the pathologist said. 'We're a bit full right now. Car crash last night on the M5. Maybe you heard about it?'

Mike nodded. 'Seven dead.'

'Yes, nasty. Anyway, here's your man.'

Mike had seen bodies pulled out of the water before, some of them so bloated and discoloured they looked scarcely human. Alastair had not been immersed that long, but the rocks and tide had done their own damage and the shotgun wounds had been further scraped and beaten by the tides, turning Alastair's face into a bloody pulp.

'I'd like to see his hands,' Mike said.

'Certainly. There's a ring still on the left, looks as if it's been there for a long time. A wedding band probably. They always get tight as we get older and the body gets, well, that little bit bigger.'

Mike looked closely at the dead man's hands and at

the ring that he'd seen so many times, a broad band of light yellow gold.

'Until we've got the dental records nothing's positive,' he said, 'but I believe that this is Alastair Bowen.'

'Well, if I meet up with another six-foot middle-aged male I'll let you know,' the pathologist announced with satisfaction. 'Until then we'll assume this is your man. I'll get the reports to you as soon as I can.'

Mike phoned Peterson from the mobile in his car.

'I'm pretty certain,' he told him. 'Gunshot wounds to the face, but I'm in little doubt.'

'Right,' Peterson said quietly. 'Well, that's that then. Another one chalked up.'

'Anything on the house-hunting?'

'I've people doing the rounds, and we've contacted the other agencies. You remember, there were a couple from up north and others from further along the south coast, but it's going to be pure luck if we come up with anything. Agents vary in how long they keep their records, so we're pulling the property guides from the local papers for that period as well.'

'Sounds like a long shot.'

'The man's got to live somewhere, Mike.'

Jake had taken a break for lunch. He was sitting in a roadside café finishing his tea and reading the paper when he saw Charlie's advert in the Lonely Hearts section.

He read it twice, just to be sure, then a slow smile spread across his face. So, Charlie Morrow had a sense of humour.

He tried the number from the pay phone in the café, only to have Charlie's direct line intercepted by the reception switchboard.

'I'm sorry,' the woman told him, 'he's not in his room right now, he's having his physio.'

Jake declined to leave a message. He felt somewhat put out by the delay. A call to the *Dorchester Herald* came next. 'Sorry,' he was told, 'but it's too late to place an advert for tomorrow. We usually need at least two days.'

He put the receiver down, thinking quickly. Then called the *Herald* again and asked to be put through to Ed Macey.

Macey was not at his desk and it was Liz who took the call.

'Hello, Ed Macey's desk.'

'My but your voice has changed. Are you taking anything for it?'

Liz giggled. 'Macey's not here right now,' she said. 'He'll be about ten minutes. Can I get him to call you back?'

'No, thank you, love. I won't be here by then. I'm calling to leave a message for a man called Charlie Morrow. He's got a small ad in your Lonely Hearts.'

He felt the change in Liz's attitude even before he next heard her voice and was amused as she began to stall.

'A message, you say, for Charlie Morrow. OK. Right. If you'll tell me what it is, I'll pass it on. Of course, I will.'

Jake leaned back against the wall, looking out across the café. He heard a couple of clicks on the line and guessed Liz would now be recording the call. The slight echo when he next spoke made him wonder if she'd switched to speaker phone.

'I take it you're recording this for posterity. Well, that's all right. No doubt your experts will have a lot of fun pinpointing the accent and getting it all wrong.'

'I wouldn't know,' Liz told him. 'I mean, I don't know much about those things.'

'No? Well, never mind, give yourself another year or two and I'm sure you'll be the expert Macey is. Now listen close and tell this to Charlie Morrow. I'll meet him where Marion O'Donnel died. He'll know the place I mean. And tell him if he comes alone, I'll consider giving him the child.'

'When?' Liz asked him. 'I've got to tell him when.'

'It's a sacred place, love. He'll know what time.'

'No! Wait!' Liz shouted. 'Wait, don't hang up yet. Charlie can't drive. His hands—'

'Of course. I hadn't thought of that. Well, tell . . . Ah, yes, tell Maria Lucas that she has to drive him. She'll do that for the sake of the child, I'm sure.'

He paused, enjoying the panic in Liz's voice, but also the fact that her nerve had held enough to remind him about Charlie.

'We should get together some time,' he said. 'Have a little chat, maybe take in a film, or have dinner. My place maybe? Or should it be yours?'

Macey was mortified that he'd not been the one to take the call, but listening to the tape he had to admit that Liz had done well.

'You OK?' he asked her. She was smoking again, he noted. Probably not a good sign.

'Sure I am. Sure. I just got off the phone from talking to a murderer. He invited me to dinner. How the hell'm I supposed to feel?'

'Make him take you somewhere special,' Macey advised, realizing even as he said it that he'd gone too far. He patted Liz's shoulder in his usual parody of comfort and dug a packet of cigarettes from the bottom of his drawer. 'Here, love, I'm sorry,' he said. 'And there aren't many people hear me say that in one lifetime.'

Charlie was as excited as Macey, but worried too.

'He won't keep the appointment,' he said. 'It's all just one big joke to him, seeing us running round in circles. I've got to get on to Mike. He'll never agree to Maria driving me.'

'Don't see he'll have much choice,' Macey said. 'She's a lady with a mind of her own and she'd do anything to get that little girl back. Charlie, this place he's talking about?'

'It's a place called West Kennet. Other side of Devizes.'

'And presumably he means midnight as the meeting time. Do we have to bring them in on this . . . Sorry, stupid question. OK, you get on to Peterson. But, Charlie, you cut me out of this and I'll never let you rest, you know that, don't you?'

Chapter Twenty-Eight

It was something like a two-hour drive from Honiton to Devizes they had estimated and West Kennet was just a little further on. There was no village there, only a cottage, a gate leading to a path between ploughed fields and, at the top of a steep hill, the long barrow itself silhouetted against the skyline.

'I've not seen the place since last winter,' Charlie told Maria as they drove. 'It's a bleak spot at the best of times and I won't forget that night in a hurry. Tipping it down with rain, visibility a few feet and this red-hot shell of a burnt-out car that just wouldn't cool, no matter what Mother Nature chucked at it.'

'He won't be there, will he?' Maria said. 'And what he said about letting Essie go, that's not true either, is it?'

Charlie looked at her. She was staring straight ahead, trying to concentrate on the road, but her hands gripped the wheel so tightly he could see the bones of her knuckles through the skin.

'He knew what he was about when he said you had to drive, didn't he? I wish I didn't have to put you through this, love.'

'I know, Charlie. It's just we're none of us fooled by this, we know it's just another Jake Bowen line, and yet—'

'We can't afford not to go, just in case he plays it straight with us this time.'

Charlie shifted uncomfortably in his seat. He didn't find it easy to be anywhere for long. There was so much of him that rubbed and chafed where the new skin was growing or the scarring pulled at the surrounding skin. He took pills at night and hated doing it, but the few hours of oblivion were precious and it was the only way that he could sleep.

It had been chaos since Peterson had been told about Jake's call. He'd been furious with Macey and with Charlie himself, but his rant had been cut short by the need to act on the information. And Macey would have to wait for his exclusive.

'When we're done with this, you can write the bloody book,' Peterson had told the journalist. 'I'll give you rights to my frigging memoirs, but you've got to hold off on this one. If the public knows he's making fools of us yet again then all the cooperation we're beginning to get will come to nothing. And we'll still be no nearer finding that child.'

Macey had agreed to back off, albeit reluctantly. 'But anyone else gets so much as a whiff of this,' he promised, 'and I'll publish the whole damn thing, with or without your cooperation. You mark my words on that.'

Kennet was way outside Peterson's jurisdiction. Charlie had been a serving officer on the local force when he'd been injured and the help they had received had been unstinting. An ARV had been in place since before Maria had collected Charlie. There were officers in the cottage beside the gate that led to the barrow and still others at the monument itself. An unmarked car with a young couple in plain clothes sat in the lay-by fifty yards up the road and officers equipped with night sights were stationed at vantage points all around the area.

Peterson and his opposite number from Devizes had taken up position in the shadows of Silbury Hill, the giant earthworks that faced the West Kennet long barrow across the Devizes road.

Mike was following Maria's car with two armed officers.

It was a massive operation. Charlie wondered how much it was costing and what must be going through Jake's mind when he set it up. He wondered too what Maria was thinking just then, but he found he couldn't ask. Probably the same hopeless thoughts that were going through his own mind.

'We're almost there,' he commented as they reached the traffic island a little over a mile from their destination. The Wagon and Horses pub was in darkness and the unlit road curved ahead and out of sight. 'Just take it slow,' he said, 'or you'll miss the pull-in. It's not well marked.'

Maria dropped her speed. In the mirror she could see Mike's car a good way behind. He had orders to go past her when she parked up, then stop further along the road. She saw Silbury looming out of nowhere on the left, just before Charlie told her they'd arrived and pointed to the lay-by on the right-hand side.

'Well, now we're here,' she said, her voice unsteady for all that she tried to remain in control, 'what do we do?'

'It's ten to twelve,' Charlie said. 'We get out and walk to the place where Marion O'Donnel died and then we wait.' And when it's plain the bastard isn't here, he thought, I suppose we turn ourselves around and go back the way we came.

Miles away, Jake had the windows open and if he listened hard he could hear the sea. He'd been watching the late film, an old B-movie horror flick, the sort he'd grown up with and still loved, where the heroines scream so prettily and threaten to fall out of their clothes and evil can be destroyed by a cross and a sharp stick.

He sipped his beer and thought about Charlie Morrow and all his entourage waiting for him in the dark in the middle of nowhere.

'Next time, Charlie,' he whispered to himself, highly amused by his little escapade. Anyway, he thought, it wouldn't be so bad. At least this time the rain had stayed away.

Chapter Twenty-Nine

It was eight o'clock on the Friday morning. Mike figured he'd had less than an hour's sleep, but somehow rest would not come. His mind was running in all directions, refusing to either make sense or be still. He felt more deeply depressed than he could ever remember, except perhaps when Stevie had died. Nothing had as yet quite matched that, but the way he felt now came very close.

Beside him Maria slept. She'd cried herself to sleep, having kept a hold on her emotions until they'd been alone. She had driven back with Peterson in stony silence, then finally broken down. It was a revelation to him. Maria never cried, was always in control, always the one to give comfort. It was the final confirmation of just how hopeless their situation seemed.

The only compensation he could find was gratitude, that she trusted him enough to let him see how utterly bereft she felt.

'I dreamed of calling Jo,' she'd told him, 'and telling her that Essie was safe and it was all over. I knew I was just kidding myself, Mike, but it was something to hang on to, you know.'

'You'll still get to do that,' he told her. 'It will be all right.'

And she'd been kind enough not to tell him to his face that he was a liar.

It was almost two weeks since Essie had disappeared from her school and they were no further on.

He must have dozed again despite himself, because the next time he looked at the clock it was almost nine. The bedroom window was open and sounds from the street filtered in: traffic noise and people's voices as they went about their day. He lay still, nagging at the random thoughts still plaguing him, then he turned over and woke Maria.

'We're going to talk to Max,' he told her. '*You're* going to talk to Max. We have to know where Jake bought his house.'

It was early afternoon by the time they got to the prison and Max was in flirtatious mood. Maria was a beautiful woman and Max liked attractive females, though he was fickle when it came to type. His last preference had been for blondes, but he was quite prepared to change his mind.

'Nice of you to brighten my day, Inspector Croft,' he said. 'But you'll excuse me if I ask what the lady sees in you. She could take her choice, if you ask me.'

Maria raised an eyebrow at Mike but she returned Max's smile. 'I suppose I don't always like the obvious,' she said.

'Nice answer, yes, nice answer. It's good to look at the unusual. Jake always said you should try and view the familiar from an unfamiliar angle. That way you learn to see things as they really are.'

'And does that work for you, Mr Harriman?'

Jane Adams

'Oh, call me Max. It's not often that I get the choice. But to answer your question, yes, I find it works for me. People are so hidebound, don't you think?'

Maria nodded. 'Probably,' she said. 'Sometimes people have big ambitions, big ideas, but reality gets in the way of achieving them. I think, for most of us, our families and the need to earn a living end up taking priority over the rest.'

Max shook his head. 'I never wanted that,' he said. 'Family, it just ties you down. It's better to be free of all of that.'

Maria nodded slowly. 'I used to think that way,' she said, 'but it can get lonely sometimes. You never wanted someone special in your life, Max? Someone who thought you were the most important thing in the world?'

Max grinned at her. 'He thinks that way about you, does he? I'm not surprised. You're quite a catch for a humble copper.'

Maria laughed. 'I'll keep reminding him of that. But did you never want that for yourself?'

Max narrowed his eyes and contemplated the question. 'Just what is it you want from me?' he asked Maria. 'I mean, this is very nice and I'm quite happy to waltz around the question all the day, but I'm curious just the same.'

'What do you think I've come for?'

'The same thing all of them ask for. Tell me about Jake, they say. What did Jake do? What did Jake say? And I understand the fascination, I really do. My whole life has been spent looking at what Jake has done with his and trying to get close, even within touching distance, of half that he's achieved.'

'But sometimes you'd like to be valued for yourself,' Maria stated. 'I think that's natural, Max. Everyone would want that.'

Max scratched his head, then got up and began to pace around the room. From the corner, Mike observed, content to let things take their course for a while. He watched Maria shifting into her professional role, the change in her almost physical as she moved back mentally into her working clothes, and she said nothing as Max paced the room, gathering his thoughts. It seemed like a long time before he sat down and began to talk again.

'Has he got rid of that father of his yet?'

'I wouldn't know,' Maria lied smoothly. Confirmation of Alastair's death had not yet hit the news. 'Do you think he might?'

'Oh, yes,' Max told her. 'Why else would he take Alastair away?'

'It's your story, you tell me.'

'No, if Jake's got him, then it's a dead story now. It doesn't matter any more.'

'What does matter?' Maria asked him. 'What would matter now?'

Max thought about it for a while, then said, 'Perfection. Getting things the best they possibly could be. Nothing else was good enough for Jake. Pushing the envelope, was how he put it. Always pushing the envelope.'

He glanced over at Mike, then, turning his attention

back to Maria, said, 'Jake, now, he never went for that family thing. He'd seen his own lot, where that got them. Jake wanted more than that. He wanted a place of his own, away from the back streets, somewhere he could breathe. And a studio. Somewhere bright and airy he could work. He wanted to retire at forty-five and live in luxury the rest of his days. Somewhere warm, with open skies and blue seas. And he wanted to be famous. To be admired for his work. For what he had achieved.'

Maria held her breath. The mention of a house seemed almost too perfect. 'Did he get all of those things?' she asked him. 'We know about the flat in London of course, you told us that, but does that fit with Jake's dreams?'

'Oh, that. That was just convenient. That wasn't what Jake wanted, only somewhere to send post and for people to stay. Jake had his own place and his own life quite apart from that.'

'Did you ever go there? To Jake's other place?'

Max awarded her a pitying look. 'Do you think I'd tell you even if I had?' he asked. 'Honestly, you really think I'm thick or what?'

She was losing it, Maria realized. She'd tried to push him far too fast. In an attempt to salvage things, she asked, 'And you, Max, did you ever dream of a place like that? A place in the sun with blue seas all around?'

But Max just laughed at her. 'You think you're oh so clever, don't you, love? But you're not. None of you are. You just go on your blinkered way, hoping for the best, and Jake runs rings around you all.'

He would say nothing after that. Maria tried once

more to draw him out but he just sat in silence, listening to her with a slight half-smile hovering around his mouth. Maria wanted to claw it off his face, to rant and scream and demand that he helped them, but she knew that it would do no good. Finally she stood up and Mike did the same. 'We're going now,' she said. 'Goodbye, Max.'

She gave him a moment when she reached the door, time to change his mind, but Max didn't so much as move.

When they got out to Mike's car she sat in the front seat and cried, tears of anger and of pain for Essie.

'Do you think he really knows?' Mike asked her when she'd calmed a little.

Maria shook her head. 'We were stupid even to imagine he would,' she said. 'Think about it, Mike. If you wanted to keep something hidden, would you tell a blabbermouth like Max? Someone who worshipped your shadow? No, he'd know Max would only want to boast about it – Jake having got his dream. Max Harriman doesn't know where Jake is. He doesn't know a damn thing.'

Back at Honiton, Mike found his desk piled high with house agents' details and back issues of property pages covering the relevant years. Two officers were already working their way through the stack, marking with highlighter anything that looked as though it matched their brief.

Most of the notices in the London flat were for the

south coast, in the main not much further west than Dorset and to the east as far as Kent. There were a few for the Yorkshire coast and Moors, but as Jake's most recent activity was all more southerly-based, they were giving priority to these and leaving the northern cottages aside.

Peterson was not in sight. Mike knew that he had to come clean about their trip to see Max. Maria was a civilian, personally involved, and the whole trip an impulse that had come to nothing. Peterson was not likely to be impressed.

But the Chief Superintendent had other things on his mind. 'I've got the path. reports on Alastair,' he said. 'It's definitely him, dental records are a match. He died of the gunshot wounds, no sign of drugs or other injury. And he'd eaten a meal three or four hours before he died. Last meal for the condemned man? Or was Jake planning on keeping him alive and then changed his mind?'

Mike shrugged, not really caring either way any more. 'We're not likely to find out,' he said, 'unless we find Jake.'

They went back into the incident room. Several dozen people, sorting information, inputting data, generating more and more facts and figures and suppositions. Maria was sitting at Mike's desk, leafing through the London faxes once again. 'He's got to be close to the sea,' she said. 'Just from the way Alastair was found.'

'Or he might easily have taken the body and dumped it over a cliff. We've got the coastguard trying to estimate a point of entry, looking at the currents and tides,' Mike commented.

'But about a third of the house details are for coastal properties. Lots of them have "ocean view" or "sea view" or "cliff-top location" as part of their selling blurb.'

'But it leaves about two-thirds of them that did not,' Peterson pointed out. 'Look, I admit it would be nice to narrow it down, but right now I'm not sure we can risk doing that.'

Maria was not going to be put off. 'Max talked about Jake loving the ocean,' she said. 'About his dreams of an open view and a clear sky.'

'He was talking about a retirement place,' Mike argued. 'Somewhere warm, he said.'

'There's something we haven't taken account of yet,' Peterson noted.

'What's that?'

'A private sale. Jake might have seen the house in the small ads. My daughter bought hers that way. In fact, I'm not even sure they even advertised it. The previous owner just put a board up outside the house with a phone number on it. She spotted it when she was out one day and the whole thing was done without an agent.'

'Well, we can pull in all the small ads that appeared in the local papers,' Mike said. 'Though it just adds to the mountain of stuff to plough through. And we'll just have to hope that Jake wasn't as observant as your daughter.'

The late afternoon sun turned the sea to fire on the horizon. Mike and Peterson had called a briefing –

'assembling the troops', as Peterson called it – to see what the day had achieved.

Maria left them to it, needing to get away from the hothouse atmosphere of the incident room. She drove down to the coast road, in places not much more than a narrow trackway, and finally pulled her car to the side of the road on the top of a grassy cliff.

It was another magnificent day. She loved weather like this, bright days at the beginning of summer, when the land was still green and the dustiness of August seemed a long way off.

She sat on the grass beside her car, gazing far out to sea, the lazy crash of waves sounding below her as she tried to imagine Jake Bowen and where he was. How different was his view from hers? Did he see the same ships far out on the horizon, the same waves, the same sunlight burning on the water?

Peterson had been talking to the coastguard. An aerial survey had been proposed using a police helicopter and the coastguard flight. In the course of the afternoon, he had come round to Maria's way of thinking about Jake. That he must be right on the coast in view of the sea. Somewhere he could have pitched Alastair's body into the ocean without the risk of being overlooked.

'Do you know how many miles of coast that is?' Peterson had asked Maria.

She didn't, and for that matter neither did he. She worried now that she might be wrong; that Peterson would put the time and effort into this and waste it all when he could be looking somewhere else.

But it was no good feeling guilty, Maria told herself.

They had to begin somewhere and, deep down, her instincts told her she was right.

A few miles along the coast, Jake stepped through the gate with Essie in his arms. She was half awake and crying, confused and frightened by this strange man who, for most of the time, seemed to be part of her bad dreams.

Jake carried the child easily. She weighed little and was still too doped to struggle very much, though she blinked in the sudden light and tried to turn her face away.

It was a wonderful day, Jake thought. The bright blue sky and silver-painted sea below, almost too bright to look at, like a mirror reflecting the sunlight. He laid the child upon the soft grass at the edge of the cliff and looked down at her, fascinated by the way the sunlight was absorbed by the darkness of her skin: the odd lights and colours, and a tonal quality white skin did not have. He turned his head this way and that, an artist assessing his subject, and what treatment he should use to give it life.

Then he bent abruptly, seizing the child by one arm and one small ankle, and lifted her high into the air, swinging her out over the surging water.

Essie was aware enough to scream, her body twisting in his hands as she reached frantically, grabbing at the empty air.

Chapter Thirty

It was close to midnight. The sky an inky blue, flecked with silver stars. Mike stood, gazing out of the window as behind him Maria put the telephone receiver down. She had been talking to Jo in spite of the late hour. Jo never slept anyway these days.

Two hours north, Max Harriman lay dozing on his bed, his thoughts and dreams filled with Jake and the high places he had loved even as a child. His dreams remembered Jake standing at the very edge of a barren granite cliff: grey clouds, grey sea, grey headland beneath Jake's feet; his arms spread wide as though he could lay himself upon the wind and fly.

Macey and Liz sat by his office desk, neither of them inclined to go home, the whisky bottle set between them slowly diminishing as the night passed.

'You ever been married, Macey?' Liz had asked.

'No, never have.'

'You ever wanted to?'

'You offering?'

Liz giggled. 'I don't think I'm right for you,' she said.

*

Sitting on the edge of his bed in a darkened room, Charlie Morrow tried to think of ways to sleep without the pills he was holding in his hand. He had just poured water into the glass and tipped out the little white pills when the telephone rang.

'We should talk, Charlie,' Jake Bowen said, and in the background Charlie heard a small child crying.

Macey stared accusingly at the telephone on his desk when it began to ring. 'Who the hell at this time of night?'

It was Charlie, excited and confused, as close to panic as Macey could imagine he would ever get.

'He's called again, Macey.'

'Then phone the bloody police.' He reached and switched on the speaker phone so Liz could hear.

'I can't. He says he'll kill Essie if I do and I believe him.'

'The kid's already dead, Charlie, we both know that.'

'No. No, she's not. Listen, he had her talk to me. Poor little bugger sobbing for her mum. He says he'll trade, me for the child, and I've got to go along with it. You must see that.'

'Charlie, Charlie, you're not thinking straight. Hold on to yourself. It's a recording he's got. The kid's dead and that's how you'll end up if you chase this.'

'I've got to take that chance.' The sound of Essie's crying had affected him as nothing else could.

'Think, Charlie,' Macey demanded again. 'You're a bloody copper, for fuck's sake. This isn't the way to go.'

He paused, waiting for Charlie's response, sensing that his initial panic was now starting to subside. 'Look, I can be with you in less than an hour. Don't do anything till I get there. Promise me that.'

'I don't know if I can. He said he'd be back in touch and I can't predict what he's going to do.'

'Just hold on. I'll be there.'

Macey put the phone down before Charlie could say another word. He turned to Liz.

'Get hold of Mike Croft, his mobile number's in the book. If you can't reach them that way, call the pub and keep it ringing till someone answers. I'm going to Charlie.'

'Are you legal?' Liz asked him, pointing at the whisky bottle.

'God knows,' Macey told her, then he was gone.

Charlie Morrow waited in his room staring at the telephone until he could no longer bear the sight of it. He switched on the computer and began to write a note addressed to Macey and to Mike, recording everything he could remember from Jake's telephone call. All that had been said or that he had heard in the background or gained an impression of.

There was a tapping on his bedroom window, french doors opening onto the garden. Charlie opened the door. Jake stood outside.

'Coming, Charlie?' he asked.

'I'll get my coat.'

'Be quick then.'

Jake watched him as he crossed the room and took his raincoat from the wardrobe. Charlie took a second while his hands where out of sight to remove his watch and press the button to set the timer, then he dropped it on the desk as he passed by. Macey would at least know how long he'd been gone. Some kind of lifeline for a drowning man.

By the time Macey arrived, Liz had done her job and the local police were already there expecting him.

'DI Croft said you might show up,' the sergeant in charge told him. 'You'd better come and look at this, but don't touch anything.'

Macey thought he was well beyond the need to be told that, but he let it pass and followed the officer down the hall.

'He went out through the french windows,' the sergeant told him, 'and someone heard a car engine start up about the time we think he left.'

'Charlie couldn't drive,' Macey said, 'he could barely close his hands to pick up a cup.'

'He could use the keyboard on the computer.'

'Well, yes, he could pick away at it with two fingers if that's what you mean, but that's a lot less control than it would take to drive a car. Jake came for him, that's obvious, isn't it?'

Macey crossed to the computer and read the brief message Charlie had typed on screen. It was full of spelling mistakes and typos and obviously been done at speed. It recounted what Macey already knew. Jake's phone call, and the crying child and then Charlie's guess that Jake's next contact might be in person and too soon for anyone to help.

'I'll set the timer on my watch,' the message said. 'You can draw some conclusion from how long I have been gone and work out how long it took for him to get here since he called me. I listened as closely as I could and there was no car engine, no sound at all in fact, except I think I heard a clock chiming in the background. The line was clear, no breaking up, and you know what mobiles can be like around here, so he must have called from somewhere the reception was good. I think for certain he must have called from home. I know it isn't much, but anything might help.'

'The watch?' Macey asked, then saw it on the desk. Macey compared it to his own.

'I took his call at ten to midnight,' Macey said, and he looked expectantly at the officer.

'It was twenty past by the time it had been relayed to us. Another ten before we made it here.'

'Which gives a forty-minute window for Jake to get here and take Charlie away.'

He looked at the message on the screen, remembering that he'd watched Charlie type. His hands were becoming more useful all the time but even so it was a slow process. He held his hands above the keyboard and pretended to input the words, Charlie-style, two fingers at a time and having to look to see each letter. It would have taken quite some time, Macey calculated. Just how long?

'The car, you say, was heard, it left here around twenty past the hour?'

The sergeant nodded, somewhat reluctantly, Macey thought.

'Looks like you just bloody missed him,' he said.

Chapter Thirty-One

Jake had bound Charlie's wrists with ducting tape and used more tape to wrap around both Charlie and the seat to keep him from moving.

Essie lay in the rear of the car, dressed only in the pink T-shirt she had been wearing for the past two weeks. Her hands and ankles were tied and a piece of tape covered her mouth. Charlie had seen her face as he'd been pushed into the car, frightened brown eyes begging him to help.

'What are you going to do with her?' he asked Jake. 'You said you'd let her go. Gave me your word.'

'And you trusted me. Now that is touching.'

'Yes,' Charlie told him. 'I did.'

Jake drove in silence for a few minutes more, clearing the side road that led from the nursing home and turning back onto the main dual carriageway. At this time of the morning it was all but empty. Charlie waited, not certain what was safe to say. Jake drove another mile before pulling the car to an abrupt halt at the side of the road.

'What are you doing?' Charlie asked him, his mouth suddenly dry.

'Letting her go,' Jake replied. 'Here looks as good a place as any.'

He was out of the car before Charlie could say a word and had lifted the child from the back seat.

'I'll untie her hands and feet,' he told Charlie, 'wouldn't want her to roll into a ditch and not get out.'

'You can't just leave her there. She's only a child.'

'Oh, I thought you wanted me to let her go?'

'Of course I do, but not here. It's a major road.'

'Well, she's more likely to be seen then, isn't she?' Jake said. 'Or I could change my mind?'

Charlie dared say nothing more. At least, he thought, the child was free. He had to hope she'd have the sense to stay off the road.

He could see her in the wing mirror as Jake moved off, sitting by the roadside, the tape still across her mouth and the look of terror in her eyes.

'You see, I always keep my promises,' Jake told him as they drove away.

When Jake next stopped the car Charlie could hear the ocean through the open door. Jake left him for a brief while and returned with a sawn-off shotgun in his hands. He took a knife from his pocket and cut the tape that bound Charlie to the seat, then stood back and let him struggle free.

'This way.'

The gun directed Charlie along a narrow crazy-paved path between borders filled with flowers. The air was cool and sweet. Charlie could just make out a white-washed house. The door was open and a soft light burned inside.

They entered through the kitchen, a large square room with windows on two sides and another door leading through to a narrow hall. There were stairs going up and other stairs going down through yet another door of painted wood that could have passed for an understairs cupboard. Charlie had to duck his head to go through, but then the passage ceiling grew to more than normal height as it passed below the stairs. He counted fourteen steps, then another open door. The gun was tight against his back now as Jake reached around and switched on the light. Fluorescent beams blinded Charlie for a moment and he almost fell down the two steps just inside the door. He blinked rapidly, trying to adjust, and Jake prodded him with the gun to move him forward, then closed the door and sat down on the higher of the two steps.

The room was empty but for a mattress on the floor. Through another door, Charlie could glimpse a toilet and wash bowl and he noted that the room was warm. A vent overhead was feeding in heated air from the rooms above.

'Finished looking?' Jake asked him, smiling at Charlie.

'There isn't much to see.'

'Oh, I don't know.' From the pocket of his jacket Jake produced the digital camera he so loved to use and raised it to his eye, the gun resting across his lap but one hand still in contact with the trigger. 'Now strip,' Jake ordered.

Frank Bennet and his wife were not used to being out so late, but they were going to a family wedding and Frank's shift pattern meant they'd had to start out late in order to get there for the Saturday morning. Em had managed to sleep a little while Frank was out at work, so she drove while Frank dozed in the partly reclined seat beside her.

She didn't like night-driving very much but it did have the advantage, she thought, that there was no one else around and she was so looking forward to her niece's wedding.

Music played softly on the radio, something soft and classical that Em recognized from an advert on TV. She was in a relaxed mood, paying little attention to the road ahead. When the tiny apparition appeared in its little pink T-shirt her first reaction was to scream and swerve the car onto the grass verge, missing the hedge and ditch by inches.

Frank woke from his doze in equal shock.

'What the hell, woman? What did you do?'

He thought she must have fallen asleep at the wheel and blundered off the road.

'A child, Frank, a little girl. She's on the road.'

Jake was fascinated by the scars on Charlie's body. He'd made him remove his clothes and even the pressure bandages that wrapped his upper body and his arms until finally Charlie stood naked in the centre of the room.

And Jake had filmed him, recorded every inch of Charlie's frame, like a sculptor admiring his handiwork.

'Did it hurt you, Charlie? Does it hurt you now?' he asked. 'Can you tell me how it feels to let so much of you burn and shrivel. What is it like when people stare at you, wondering what happened to you and if it's catching? Tell me about it. I want to know.'

For a brief time, Charlie put up with this humiliation, fear of the gun keeping him in his place. Then he grew sick of it, decided that Jake was going to kill him anyway and, if he was going to die, then he was going to do it with his clothes on and his dignity intact. He bent, picked up his shirt and began to put it on.

Jake lowered the camera. 'What are you doing, Charlie?'

'Getting dressed. You've had your money's worth, the side-show's closing.'

'I don't think I've finished.'

'Don't you? Well, I have. You've got me here because of that baby and you've freed her now. God willing, she'll be all right. You want to kill me for putting my clothes on, then go right ahead. I'm not playing your stupid games any more.'

Jake smiled at him, a slow grin spreading across his face, then raised the gun level with Charlie's head.

Chapter Thirty-Two

By seven on the Saturday morning, Essie was in hospital in Swindon and Maria was with her.

She had spoken to Jo and the Kent police were driving Essie's parents down with a full escort. They should have arrived by mid-morning and Essie's ordeal, everyone hoped, would be coming to an end.

Peterson watched Maria as she sat beside Essie, stroking her hair and talking softly to her. Coming close, he crouched down beside the bed. 'I know it's a lot to ask,' he said, 'but anything she can tell you now that might give us some clue?' Peterson knew all too well that once the parents arrived it would be impossible. They'd just want to get away from it all and it might be weeks before they allowed the police to talk to the child again.

'I'm doing what I can,' Maria reassured him. 'I want to get Charlie back as much or more than anyone. He saved Essie's life, I'm sure of that.'

Macey was already in his office. Looking at Liz, he wondered if she'd even left since last night. She looked as exhausted as he felt. He was desperately trying to knock the story into shape, ready for the early afternoon edition, and it would be passed to the news agencies, maybe even direct to one or other of the nationals after news of Essie's release and Charlie's trade broke on the breakfast shows.

Peterson had authorized Macey to release the entire story, hoping that it would capture the public imagination and shake something loose.

Liz was deeply upset about it all. She was relieved for Essie and her family, but had been crying for Charlie most of the night and her eyes were red and sore.

At eight fifteen Mike arrived. He'd already spoken to Maria and had something to add to Macey's story.

'Essie told us they were near the sea,' he said. 'We want that released, so we're passing it straight to the media across the board, but Peterson said you were to have the full version now and play it for all it's worth. Jake took her out of the house and onto the clifftop. She remembers him carrying her and thinks it was only a short way, through a garden. He held her over the water and she saw the sea below her, a long way down. He had hold of her only by an arm and a leg and she thought he was going to let her fall. She thought she was going to die.'

'Oh, God,' Liz said.

Macey was silent for a moment. 'I'm assuming you want me to quote that in full,' he said.

By ten Mike was conducting the morning briefing. A grid-pattern search by helicopter had been assigned, shadowed by those on the ground. The search was concentrating on the miles of coastline, each unit taking a number of properties gleaned from the guides and estate agents' details Jake might have used five years before.

'You're probably looking for a lone male,' Mike reminded them. 'Though we can't rely on that. You have basic descriptions in the written brief, but you must remember that Jake Bowen changes his appearance to suit. The properties on your lists are all well off the main roads, some very isolated, so the slightest sign of trouble and you call for back-up. We want no heroics and no more dead officers.'

He waited, letting his gaze travel around the room and hoping that his words were sinking in.

'Questions?'

There were a few, but everyone was eager just to be getting on.

'Remember,' Mike emphasized as the meeting broke up and he was worried by the slightly gung-ho attitude he sensed in the room, 'you call in every location as you get there and the result immediately you've got one. I want to know where each and every officer is at all times. We've got armed units standing by all along the coast road. Don't hesitate to call on them.' He gestured to the stack of strike-proof vests on a nearby table. 'They're to be worn,' he said. 'I know it's hot and I know they impede you, but we've got enough dead to bury without adding to their number.'

He watched the men and women assigned to him file out of the incident room, knowing that this scene was being repeated all along the coast. Road-blocks had been set up. Jake Bowen had to be somewhere close by. They just had to find him.

Please God, he thought, let's finish this today.

Jake watched as the helicopter flew overhead for the second time that morning, then he walked back, barefoot, through his garden.

He stood in his kitchen waiting for the kettle to boil and watched the mid-morning news on the portable TV. The news was full of him: Essie being found and Charlie Morrow being lost; the mobilization of every available officer up and down the coast; all leave cancelled on his behalf.

He made instant coffee – strong and black, very sweet and scalding hot. He sipped it slowly as he watched the bulletin, then took his coffee with him upstairs to his viewing room.

Charlie Morrow seemed to be asleep. Jake switched the camera angles, examining Charlie as he lay on the single bed. He pulled in to focus on the big man's face, studying the network of scars and patchily growing beard, the rough, stubbled areas between a network of red polished skin.

His breathing slow and even as he slept.

Charlie was not asleep, not deeply. He had dozed a little from time to time, but the dead silence of the sound-proofed room was not conducive to his brand of relaxation. Anyway, he found it hard to sleep at all without his pills.

Lying on the narrow bed, sensing that Jake was watching him, Charlie forced himself to keep very still, to pretend a lack of concern he could not feel. He tried not to imagine what Jake had planned for him and concentrated his thoughts on what might lie ahead should he finally get out of here.

He listened to the faint noises carried by the heating pipes, straining his ears for the slightest clue to Jake's movements above his head. He tried to imagine what the day must be like outside. Hot and dry, close enough to the sea to hear the roar of the tide, taste the tang of salt on the air and hear the cry of birds.

Lying there, fooling Jake into thinking he was still asleep, Charlie made up his mind that whatever Jake might have in mind, he wasn't going down easy.

Peterson and Maria had arrived back at the incident room in Honiton. Calls from the operational units were already coming in, each report being plotted on the maps pinned to the office walls. Mike snatched a moment to greet Maria before being called away and Peterson too was immediately swallowed up in the organized confusion.

Maria perched herself on the edge of one of the desks, suddenly surplus to requirements. The effects of the last days were beginning to catch up on her in full measure.

She wanted to crawl away somewhere and get some sleep. She wanted news to come in saying that Charlie had been found, Jake arrested and all of this was over and done with.

Staring at the red and blue pins scattered over the maps, she tried to second-guess the pattern of the search, to imagine Jake's reaction as he felt the net closing on him. Maria wondered what would happen if they reached the end of this intensive search, the close of this incredibly expensive day, and Jake had not been found.

Jake had spent a little time watching Charlie on the CCTV screens. He was not the most cooperative guest he'd ever had. He refused to beg, refused to panic, even declined to shout, and for the last two hours had remained on the mattress fast asleep.

Jake began to gather his things together: his passport in the name of John Phillips, sales rep, and a spare in another name; his credit cards and, again, a couple of others he had acquired along the way. It always amazed him how helpful and un-nosy the banks could be, provided you kept money flowing through their accounts.

He also packed a bag and stowed it ready in the boot of his car. It left one question: what to do with Charlie Morrow?

In Dorchester, Macey watched the latest bulletin on a portable television someone had brought into the office. He was booked for an interview later on that day, together with Peterson and Essie's mum. It was likely to be an emotional affair. And Macey's exclusive coverage of the story had been sold in reworked forms to no less than three of the national dailies and one of the major Sunday broadsheets. Macey had hit pay-dirt.

Liz sat down beside him, staring at the screen.

'You should be pleased,' she said. 'You could cut any deal you wanted right now. Any story you wanted to write.'

'Not any deal,' Macey said slowly. 'And not any story. The only one I want to write just now, love, would say that Charlie's safe and well.'

Liz turned to stare at him, for a moment not certain whether to believe him or not.

'You really mean that, don't you?'

'Yes,' he said. 'I really do.'

Chapter Thirty-Three

By lunch-time, Charlie had grown tired of his own silence. He lay on his back on the single bed and recited poetry, dredging from his memory the fragments of verse inflicted on him from primary school on.

He had begun, he estimated, about half an hour before, with nursery rhymes, and amazed himself with just how many he could remember. Exhausting those, he'd graduated to passages of Shakespeare he'd been forced to learn, line by line, comma by comma, in his early years at grammar school.

'Tomorrow and tomorrow and tomorrow ... You hear me, Jake? Quite an actor I could have been, given half the chance. Fancied myself as Hamlet, but I didn't fit the tights. You listening to me, Jake? I'll bet you are.' He paused a moment, waited for a response. 'You going to get your arse down here and talk to me, or what? You're a lousy host, you know that? You don't come down here, Jake, it won't be just the poetry. I might be forced to sing.'

Mike was at the road-block on the Dorchester road when Macey finally caught up with him.

'Rumour is you've had a couple of false alarms?'

'I won't ask where the rumour came from. There's been nothing concrete, Macey.'

'Mind if I tag along when you leave here.'

'You'd follow me if I said no.'

'Damn right I would. I'm going nuts back there.' He hesitated for a moment before asking, 'You think he's dead?'

'I don't know, Macey. Depends what Jake had in mind.'

'I keep thinking, you know, if I'd got there sooner—'

'There's nothing you could have done.'

'I'm not certain I believe that.'

'What you believe, Macey, quite frankly doesn't matter. We got Essie back and we'll find Charlie Morrow. Jake's been calling the shots long enough.'

Macey watched him walk back to his car, shoulders set square against argument. 'You really believe that, do you, Inspector Croft?' he asked. 'Or doesn't what you think matter any more either?'

By one p.m. Jake had decided it was time to leave. He listened in to Charlie's monologue one last time – the microphones he'd rigged up fed the sound through to the viewing room.

Charlie was singing a very unmusical rendition of something from Gilbert and Sullivan. He seemed to know only about half the words, making up the rest as he went along. Jake listened for a short while, amused at Charlie's version of the sorrow of a policeman's lot, wondering how long Charlie's change of mood would last and slightly regretful that he would not be hanging around long enough to find out. He switched off the basement sound and left his prisoner totally alone. The appeal of killing Charlie was just not there if there wasn't time to set it up properly and film the action. In Jake's philosophy, if you couldn't do things right, they were often better left undone. He put the rest of his essential gear into the car and left the house, he thought, for ever.

Chapter Thirty-Four

Jake got all of half a mile, driving down the single-track lane towards the main road, before being met by a police car on its way up. He was forced to back up the way he'd come, the police car following closely and finally parking across the exit from Jake's yard.

'Can I help you, officers,' Jake asked. 'I hope it won't take long. I was about to go out.'

'Anything special, sir? Maybe you could phone if you're going to be late for an appointment?'

'No, nothing special.'

'Well, then, if we could just step inside?'

Jake gave in as gracefully as he could, relieved he'd stowed his luggage in the boot and not on the back seat of his car. One officer followed him inside. Jake glanced back, curious as to what the other might be doing. He was speaking into his pocket phone, consulting a map and a list which he'd taken from the car.

The call came in to Honiton that a double-crewed unit had another possible. The third so far.

'Lone male, fits the general description, sir, and he seems a bit edgy.'

'Who wouldn't be?' Peterson questioned. 'OK, give

me the location and I'll put the nearest back-up on stand-by.'

Peterson listened, matching the details to the grid reference. The property was right slap-bang on the coast. He signed off, prepared to call the other units in.

'What's this all about?' Jake asked the officer who'd followed him inside.

'Have you seen the news today?'

'About the policeman and the little girl? Yes. Yes, I have.'

The other officer joined them now, moving to the other side of the small kitchen as though wanting to keep Jake in full view. Jake realized that he was being far too stiff, that they were not at ease with him. He tried to compensate.

'Can I offer you some tea?'

'That would be nice, but what we'd really like to do, if it's not too much bother, is to check your basement.'

Jake filled the kettle from the kitchen tap, his back to both the men. It was on the tip of his tongue to ask them where their warrant was. Instead he lied as smoothly as he could. 'I'm sorry, officer, but I don't have a basement here.'

He plugged the kettle into the socket and began to turn, then saw that what he'd taken for a list in the policeman's hand were house agents' details – a photo-copy of the write-up he'd seen when first he'd come looking at the house.

'It says here, sir, that this house has a full-sized base-ment. Have you had it sealed or filled in?'

The lunch-time washing up was still stacked on the draining board, including the sharp knife Jake had used. It was more impulse than thought that made him snatch it and he lunged forward, then slashed across the body of the nearest man, the blade catching the man's sleeve and deflecting upward, opening his cheek. Then he was out of the kitchen door and into the narrow hall.

Mike took Peterson's call just after leaving the road-block.

'It could be nothing, Mike. We've had two false ones already and brought them in, but it's not going to amount to much.'

Mike took the reference and checked it against his own map. He was about five miles away. 'On my way,' he said.

He ran to his car, shouting at Macey to join him.

'It might be nothing,' he said, 'but it's the best fit we've had so far.'

He'd slammed into gear and taken off before Macey had time to fasten his seat-belt.

'You think this is it?' Macey asked him. 'God Al-mighty, do you always drive like this?'

Mike didn't trouble to answer, too intent on taking a thirty-mile bend at twice that speed. Macey too fell silent, thinking about Charlie Morrow and visualizing his next by-line.

*

It took Jake only seconds to descend the basement steps and unlock the cellar door. The gun he'd used earlier had been propped beside it, left loaded but broken. Jake snapped it closed and then he was inside, with Charlie at gunpoint, and heading back towards the stairs.

The uninjured officer met him three steps from the top, and then he saw the gun.

'Back off,' Jake ordered him. 'I can kill this one and still have another barrel left for you.'

They moved slowly to the top of the steps, the gun pressed close against Charlie's spine. The other officer, his hands raised, was trying to talk Jake down.

'This is no good, sir. Lower the weapon. I've called for reinforcements.'

'And they've a bloody long way to come, haven't they, officer?'

They were going to die, Charlie thought, and Jake was going to get away again.

The idea that Jake should escape free and clear suddenly enraged Charlie Morrow. That he could go on killing and maiming and destroying people's lives. He had to take a chance.

They were almost at the kitchen door now, the hallway cramped and overfull with the three of them. One police officer had backed up and gone through the kitchen door when Charlie made his move. He dropped and turned, came up with his hands reaching for the gun, deflecting the shot at the moment Jake fired. The two men fell, Charlie on top of Jake, struggling for control, but the younger man was stronger and he still had possession of the gun. He hit out with the rifle stock, catching Charlie's shoulder a glancing blow, and forcing him aside. Jake rolled forward, twisting his body as Charlie struggled once more to gain control. Then Jake had pinned him down, was sitting astride his legs with the gun raised and pointing straight between Charlie's eyes. Charlie thrust upward with both hands, praying to deflect the shot before he fired, but the expected explosion of sound and pain never arrived.

A look of shock spread across Jake's face and he fell forward, the knife he had used to slash the policeman's face wedged deeply in his back.

Chapter Thirty-Five

It seemed a long time before anyone arrived and when they did it was all at once. Patrol cars screaming down the lane, a helicopter hovering above them. Armed police emerging from ploughed fields, sprung from some lunatic effect-artist's dream.

Charlie had led the other officer outside, after helping him to get his injured colleague from the house and fetching the first aid kit from the police car. They sat in the garden, Charlie doing his best to clean the face wound and stop the bleeding.

'It's not as bad as it looks,' he said hopefully. 'A bit of a scar, maybe, but that's all.'

He saw the other man studying his face and then pulling his gaze away, embarrassed. 'I'll be all right,' he said. A macho man, trying not to cry.

The sun was hot on their backs but the young man who had killed Jake Bowen shivered as though freezing cold.

'What's your name?' Charlie asked him.

'George, George Mitchell. What will happen next?'

He was still a child, Charlie thought, and, now it was all over, very scared.

'You did what you had to do,' Charlie told him. 'No one can tell you anything else, believe that.'

'I feel sick, and look at me, I'm shaking like a bloody leaf.'

'You and me both,' Charlie said. 'You been in the force long?'

George Mitchell managed a weak half-smile. 'Six months out of my probationary year,' he said. 'God, what a start.'

Charlie laughed. Yeah, what a start, he thought, and it was far from over yet. There'd be the inquiry, the immediate suspension from duty, the debriefing and the counselling, and George's slow realization that he had killed a man.

'We'll get through it,' Charlie told him. 'Don't you worry, we'll get through.'

The first of the police cars arrived then, their sirens screaming through the still air. There was an ambulance, with its flashing blue light, and people everywhere, shouting instructions and running across Jake's close-clipped lawn. They broke around Charlie and the others like a flood. The injured officer was led away. Someone was trying to organize the chaos of parked and now wedged cars, and the armed officers were being stood down and lounging in the garden, waiting for someone to tell them what to do.

A senior officer came and took George Mitchell aside, quietly encouraging him to tell his story, easing him back into a system that had its own rules and its own closed door.

Charlie didn't feel a part of that any more. He ignored their questions and their anxious looks, and the ambulance man who said he was in shock and needed medical attention. It was all suddenly so alien to Charlie Morrow. Now Jake was dead, he didn't feel a part of anything.

He was standing on the cliff, looking out to sea, when Mike Croft arrived. He had Macey with him and Charlie took a moment to wonder how Macey had wangled that.

'Charlie! You OK?'

'Yeah, I'm fine. Just fine.'

As he watched, a cormorant skimmed lazily above the ocean, the same one that Jake had watched so many times. It was, Charlie thought, an inspiring sight, something unchanged for generations and still going on.

'You ever thought about what it would be like to stand here with the wind in your face and the sun on your back and then just let it go? Step over the line?'

'Charlie?' Macey's voice was scared and Charlie felt a hand gripping his arm.

'It's all right, Macey, I'm not going to jump.'

He turned away, let Macey lead him back from the edge.

'Too earthbound, Macey,' Charlie said. 'I never learned to fly.'

Afterword

Three weeks to the day after Jake Bowen's death Julia's body was finally released to her parents, and that same morning Alastair Bowen was accepted back by the community of St Bartolph's Church. He was to be cremated that afternoon, but Mike had decided not to remain for that.

He had attended the brief funeral service as the police representative, selected because he had most contact with the man during those last few days.

There were few people there, the media being kept outside and only a handful of folk wanting to be openly acknowledged as Alastair's friends sitting with him in the church. Alastair had left instructions in his will. No flowers and no hymns, just a few words spoken by a cleric who had never known him and whose eulogy could have been for anyone.

It was a sad end, Mike thought, and he was glad when it was over and he could slip away.

Outside, the press was there in force, but Mike was not the main focus of their interest. That was reserved for those who had known Alastair in life and were less able to brush the questions aside with official words. Mike was soon back in his car and ready to go.

He sat back in the driver's seat and reached for his mobile phone. Maria's number was first in the memory.

'It's all finished then?' she asked him.

Alastair's funeral, yes, but there was so much yet that wasn't over. There'd be the inquest, and the internal inquiries into what could have been managed better and what lessons had been learned. And then there was Essie. She was healing well, the memories hazed by the sedative Jake had given her, but Mike knew it was likely to be months before Jo would so much as speak to him again. She was depressed and paranoid, unable to let either of her children out of her sight. The nightmares were a torture when she slept and the waking memory pervaded every conscious hour. Jake Bowen had left a terrible legacy.

'Are you still there?' Maria asked him, he had been silent for so long.

'Yes, I'm still here. I was thinking, that's all.'

'There's a lot to think about.'

'Can I see you tonight? There's something I want to ask and I can't say it over the phone.'

She sounded surprised. 'Pick me up, seven thirty. We'll go and eat somewhere.'

They finalized arrangements and Mike switched off his phone, smiling to himself. In his pocket was a ring, an emerald, because Maria liked them, and as he started the car to drive home Mike was hoping she would say yes.

JANE ADAMS

The Angel Gateway

Macmillan   £16.99

To be published on 25 August 2000

'Kitty?' Ray said. The singing stopped and the woman half turned towards him before vanishing from his sight.

Six months after the horrific petrol-bomb attack that left him severely burned, Detective Sergeant Ray Flowers moves to his late aunt's cottage to contemplate his future. But all too soon the past darkens his stay there . . .

According to his aunt's diaries, the cottage is often frequented by a mysterious woman referred to only as 'Kitty'. But this is no ordinary visitor. For, Ray learns, Katherine Hallam once lived in the cottage – and was tried as a witch in 1643 . . .

As he searches for an explanation for his own appalling injuries, Ray becomes increasingly captivated by the ghostly young woman who, like him, bears terrible facial scars. With the help of local curate John Rivers and archive librarian Sarah Gordon he slowly pieces together her tragic tale, played out against the menacing backdrop of the English Civil War.

But what Ray cannot even begin to comprehend is the role he himself played in sealing Kitty's fate – more than three hundred years before he was born . . .

JANE ADAMS

The Greenway

Pan Books   £5.99

Cassie Maltham still has nightmares about that day in August 1975 when she and her twelve-year-old cousin Suzie took a short cut through The Greenway, an ancient enclosed pathway steeped in Norfolk legend. For somewhere along this path Suzie simply vanished . . .

Haunted also is John Tynan, the retired detective once in charge of Suzie's case, still obsessed by the tragic disappearance he failed to solve two decades ago.

Then another young girl goes missing at the entrance to The Greenway. And Cassie's nightmares take on a new and terrifying edge . . .

JANE ADAMS

Bird

Pan Books £5.99

A CHILLING TALE OF A YOUNG WOMAN'S SEARCH TO UNCOVER THE DEMONS HAUNTING HER GRANDFATHER.

After six years of separation, Marcie has come to the bedside of her dying grandfather to make her peace.

But Jack Armitage cannot achieve that peace, for he is haunted by the terrible vision of a body hanging from a tree and the ghostly image of 'Rebekkah', a woman he insists is standing beside him, a noose around her neck.

Before he dies Marcie vows to uncover the true story behind this woman. Even if it points to her grandfather being a murderer . . .

JANE ADAMS

Fade to Grey

Pan Books   £5.99

After two months' sick leave, DI Mike Croft had hoped for a simple case to ease himself back into his job. But it is not to be, for a serial rapist is stalking the streets of Norwich, targetting young blonde women. At first it seems each attack is identical. But then the forensic reports come in – and Mike is faced with a far more horrifying scenario.

Two hundred miles away in Avebury, a car is seen burning at the top of a hill. Inside is the body of a young blonde woman, identity unknown. There is no reason to suspect a connection with the Norwich rapes.

But there is a connection: the former actress Theo Howard, now living a quiet life in Norfolk. And for Theo, time is running out . . .